OCEAN PICTURES

THE GOLDEN AGE OF TRANSATLANTIC TRAVEL
1936 to 1959

Bought at the
Ocean Bookshop

Queen Elizabeth 2

RMS *Queen Mary* steams into New York.

OCEAN PICTURES

THE GOLDEN AGE OF TRANSATLANTIC TRAVEL
1936 to 1959

JANE HUNTER-COX

Webb & Bower

MICHAEL JOSEPH

First published in Great Britain 1989 by
Webb & Bower (Publishers) Limited
9 Colleton Crescent, Exeter, Devon EX2 4BY
in association with Michael Joseph Limited
27 Wright's Lane, London W8 5TZ

Penguin Books Ltd, Registered Offices: Harmondsworth, Middlesex, England
Viking Penguin Inc, 40 West Street, New York, New York 10010, USA
Penguin Books Australia Ltd, Ringwood, Victoria, Australia
Penguin Books Canada Ltd, 2801 John Street, Markham, Ontario, Canada L3R 1D4
Penguin Books (NZ) Ltd, 182–190 Wairau Road, Auckland 10, New Zealand

Designed by Vic Giolitto and Malcolm Couch

Production by Nick Facer/Rob Kendrew
Text and illustrations Copyright © 1989 Jane Hunter-Cox

British Library Cataloguing in Publication Data
Hunter-Cox, Jane.
  Ocean pictures: The golden age of transatlantic travel 1936–1959.
  1. Passenger transport. Shipping. Liners.
  I. Title.
  387.2′432

  ISBN 0–86350–250–4

Typeset in Great Britain by Scribes

Duotone reproduction produced by
Mandarin Offset, Hong Kong

Printed and bound in Hong Kong

Contents

For Stuart
with love

Map, on board both vessels, showing relative daily positions.

PART 1

OCEAN PICTURES

The Story in Brief

FASTEST OCEAN SERVICE IN THE WORLD

CUNARD

SOUTHAMPTON, CHERBOURG AND NEW YORK

R.M.S. "MAURETANIA"   R.M.S. "BERENGARIA"   R.M.S. "AQUITANIA"

Postcard showing three of the earlier Cunard liners.

Ocean Pictures

The Story in Brief

--------------- ☆ ---------------

*T*HE TITLE AND CONTENTS OF THIS BOOK were inspired by a small family-run company of the same name, which is still in operation today. Ocean Pictures was one of the early pioneers of shipboard photography, and throughout its history it has had a long and traditional association with the Cunard Line. As photographic concessionaires on board *Queen Mary* and the first *Queen Elizabeth*, the company was able to build up a unique, and so far unpublished, collection of photographs taken during the thirties, forties and fifties. During that time, the two great Queens carried the cream of international society, politicians and film stars across the Atlantic, and since no other photographers had access to these celebrities for the five-day crossing, many of the photographs are remarkably relaxed and informal. These were the golden days of transatlantic travel, the ultimate way to cross the great western ocean, before less glamorous, but more convenient, air-travel became commercially viable in the late fifties. The opportunity to record a captive audience of the rich and famous on film was a photographer's dream.

The company known as Ocean Pictures was founded in 1929 by Casimir Watkins, following a casual conversation in a bar with one of the directors of Cunard. They were travelling from America on board the *Beren-*

garia and found themselves chatting together as they enjoyed a pre-dinner cocktail. Casimir was returning to England after many months away on an expedition to South America, and he was looking forward to a well earned break at home. At that time he was a well-respected entomologist, following in the path of his father, but through the course of this timely conversation, he realized the challenge and potential of setting up his own business. Until now his photographic experience had played a supportive role in the illustration and documentation of his entomological pursuits, and had therefore provided him with the bare bones of the knowledge he would need to set up a professional operation. However, undaunted, he borrowed £500 from his uncle to finance the business and set up the first Ocean Pictures photographic concession on board the *Lancastria*. After six months he was able to repay his uncle, and at the same time set up a darkroom on board the *Berengaria*, the flagship of the Cunard fleet. In 1936 Ocean Pictures accepted the concession on the recently launched and highly prestigious *Queen Mary*.

*T*HE *BERENGARIA* WAS ORIGINALLY called the *Imperator*, she was a magnificent ship, with spectacularly rich and exotic interiors. All her fixtures and fittings were of the highest quality and

3rd Class Smoking Room

3rd Class Dining Room

R.M.S. "BERENGARIA"

CUNARD LINE

3rd Class Social Room

3rd Class 4 Berth Room

PASSENGERS WERE ENCOURAGED to use the safe at all times when travelling. Imagine, therefore, the purser's horror when he came down one morning to his office and discovered that the safe had been robbed. It transpired that when it had been removed from the *Berengaria*, only the front, top, bottom and side panels were transported, someone had forgotten to take the back panel, perhaps deliberately, as it would have been a major task to extract it from the bulkhead on the *Berengaria*. To make matters worse, instead of being bolted to a secure internal bulkhead on the *Mauretania*, it had been fixed to a thin partition wall leading directly through to a passageway. The robbery had taken place in the passageway and had been a simple operation for the burglar – he had only to tap a hole through a flimsy partition and help himself. A few heads definitely rolled subsequently, and the truth was concealed for some time afterwards.

constructed with outstanding workmanship and an old-fashioned pride in work that was built to last. This was the case with the main safe, an enormous contraption made of solid steel, that was situated in the purser's office. All the ship's documents and monies were kept inside, including the passenger's valuables. Sadly in 1938 the *Berengaria* was scrapped, mainly due to the depression, but certain items were salvaged from her and reused on other Cunard ships. The safe found its way on board the *Mauretania* and because of its massive size and weight proved to be quite tricky to install. Once in position, in the purser's office, it was soon put to good use. However, it had apparently developed little idiosyncrasies in transit, for instance the numerical dial lock on the front occasionally refused to open the door. It was so finely tuned that the motion of the ship would affect its operation, and there was many an embarrassing moment as the purser struggled behind the scenes, trying to open the unyielding door as a lady passenger waited impatiently for her jewellery.

Conditions at sea were not ideally suited to developing photographs. The constant roll of the ship, fluctuations in electrical power and ambient temperatures are not conducive to producing good results. As all photographers know, a certain amount of precision is required to maintain chemicals at a specific temperature during processing, and it is vitally important that the mixtures remain uncontaminated. This can be a tricky operation on land and so one can only imagine the difficulties associated with producing successful photographs at sea. It is commendable that the early ship's photographers consistently produced good work. The quality of the illustrative material in this book speaks for itself.

Some photographers went to extraordinary lengths to achieve perfection, and necessity being the mother

Right
An Ocean Pictures' photographer standing upright. This pose accentuates the dramatic angle of the ship's deck in heavy seas in mid-Atlantic.

Above
One for the personal album as the ship's photographer, John Dooley, is caught relaxing during deck shots.

Left
The photographer's darkroom on board the *Queen Mary*, this was one of the more spacious examples.

of invention one enterprising chap mounted his enlarger on a bed of ping-pong balls! This apparently helped to counteract the roll of the ship and enabled him to print more efficiently. The equipment in use at that time was both heavy and cumbersome. The cameras were Century Graphics (younger sisters of the famous Speed Graphics) and these performed well using five-by-four-inch sheet film. Five-by-seven-inch film was also used with the appropriate subject matter. The flash guns were carried at shoulder height and were powered by a pack resembling a small car battery which was carried with the help of a heavy-duty shoulder strap. As one photographer remembers (tongue in cheek), many a lop-sided picture was taken as the day wore on and the weight of the equipment took its toll!

During the winter months bookings on the great liners declined. As a result, many departments on board, including Ocean Pictures, cut back on staff. When the ship was booked to capacity there would be a full complement of three photographers. On many occasions four would have been useful, but the cabin allocation only accommodated three persons. Space is always at a premium on board ship, and once secured is jealously guarded. Ideally, the most suitable location for a darkroom at sea is dead amidships – half way down and half way along. This is the pivotal point of a ship where the least motion is felt, therefore the perfect site. Unfortunately for the photographic department there is always competition for this optimum position. Photographers come pretty low on the list of priorities and invariably end up in some less than ideal locations. The final site of the darkroom on the *Queen Mary* was the original Ladies Powder Room. This was situated on the starboard side behind the Observation Bar and, although fairly high up, was at least spacious as the ceiling height went through two decks. Nobody complained.

In the heyday of the Cunard Queens the crew observed a rigid set of rules and remained in crew-designated areas. For some, a glimpse of daylight and a breath of fresh air was something to be cherished. One nursing sister remembers being allowed to use a particular lift, but only when in formal uniform; she was permitted to go straight to the top deck without stopping. Photographers, by the nature of the job, were more privileged and were permitted to move around the passenger decks. However, to abuse this privilege was to lay one's job on the line, and if ever discovered in the wrong place at the wrong time one had to come up with a cast-iron excuse or face the consequences.

*I*T WAS NOT UNUSUAL for some crew members serving on passenger liners to travel the whole way from Southampton to New York without seeing the light of day. Some unfortunates went both ways without a breath of fresh air. Most crew quarters are inboard and therefore do not have portholes. The job would often entail working below the water line, or in areas where it would be impossible to have a porthole. If, during a rest period, a man chose not to visit the 'crew' deck to take in some fresh air it was quite possible for him to reach the other side of the Atlantic without realizing he had left Southampton. It is quite disorientating to wake up in the morning, in an inboard cabin, and not know whether it is morning or night. One photographer, having worked a night shift, got up in a hurry, put on his dinner jacket, black tie and cummerbund, and went down to dinner . . . only to find breakfast was being served.

Bing Crosby with his personal Ocean Pictures' photographs,
after collecting them from the darkroom on the *Queen Mary*.

BING CROSBY, although not remembered as being the most generous tipper on board, was nevertheless a popular guest. When he wanted to get away from the crowd he would slip along to the photographic darkroom, settle back into the same old chair, take out his pipe and puff contentedly on it while chatting to the photographers. He did this so often that very soon he was being roped in to help, and it wasn't unusual to find him counting photographs and numbering them. He seemed to enjoy the atmosphere and camaraderie that this small retreat provided and regularly sought the peace and relaxation so often craved by travelling celebrities. He would show his gratitude at the end of the voyage by sending a large crate of beer to the darkroom.

When an extra pair of hands was needed in the darkroom, suitable recruits were eagerly sought and members of the ship's band could often be persuaded to help out. Even early in the morning, musicians who only a few hours before had been entertaining passengers, could be found assisting with the numbering of negatives and dry-mounting the finished prints on to display boards. These boards usually accommodated a dozen photographs and at least forty boards were completed each morning, that being the average for the previous night's work. By present day standards around four hundred negatives does not seem very much, but one must remember that each time the shutter clicked, a new magazine of film had to be loaded by hand and a delay of around thirty or forty seconds was needed for the flash gun to recharge. All the processing work in the darkroom was done individually by hand. Each piece of film and each print was handled several times throughout the various stages of development and was then hung out to dry

Frances Day—a passenger on the maiden voyage of the *Queen Mary*.

FRANCIS DAY was a passenger on the maiden voyage of the *Queen Mary*. She requested that a photograph be taken of her while playing the piano. When the print was ready the photographer took it up to her suite for her approval, with another copy which he politely asked her to autograph. This she kindly consented to do but, before handing it back, took the pen and quickly scribbled across the image of herself, altering what appeared to her to be an unflattering rear view. When the result was to her satisfaction, she handed the photograph back.

NOT LONG AGO, at a society party in New York, a young gentleman was engaged in conversation with an eminent laywer. He told the story of the very beautiful lady that he had once had on his books, by the name of Mrs Helen Warwick, who was still stunning even though she was then in her eighties. She had told him that when she died, she would like him to be responsible for ensuring that her ashes would be placed in the final resting place of her choice. When the time came, he received notification from the mortuary that her ashes were ready and he opened the pre-sealed envelope with her instructions. He was asked to go to the South of France and distribute her remains over the cliffs in Nice, Monte Carlo, Cannes and at various other locations along the Riviera. After carrying out her precise instructions, he returned home and opened a second envelope. Inside, he found a letter and a cheque for £80,000. The letter thanked him for carrying out her request and was signed . . . Francis Day.

Passengers look for their photographs, taken the night before,
on the many display boards on deck.

on lines strung across the bulkheads. It took many man hours to develop the fruits of one night's work.

The rule of thumb for all photographers at sea is to get the most recent work up on display as quickly as possible; this often meant working through the night, in shifts if necessary. It became a matter of pride, as each ship's photographer compared notes, to claim the best quality and the fastest time for getting the finished work displayed and ready to sell. Photographs went on sale for five shillings and sixpence, or eighty cents, each – both currencies were accepted on board. Passengers were invariably amazed to see themselves in photographs taken only hours before as they wandered out of the breakfast dining-room. The display boards were put up in three different sections of the ship; first class, cabin class and tourist class. It was very easy to identify the photographs from the background interiors and by the style of dress worn by the guests portrayed. In many cases it was easy to spot the invaders from the lower decks in incorrect dress. These pictures would be weeded out from the first-class boards and displayed in tourist class where, predictably, they always seemed to sell! Some passengers, in later years on the *QE2*, disbelieving that there was a darkroom on board, were hoodwinked into visiting the helicopter deck at 5:30 am on the understanding that films were airlifted off each day to be processed ashore and the finished prints returned to the ship each day. Many gullible passengers fell victim to this ruse. There was one in particular who came up to the sales desk rather dejectedly one morning saying that he had waited up on deck for two hours and hadn't seen the helicopter arrive, did this mean that there would be no photographs on display today?

THERE WERE VERY STRICT RULES governing the movement of passengers from tourist and cabin class into the first-class dining-rooms. Problems would arise when gentlemen travelling first class would form an attachment with attractive ladies travelling tourist or cabin class. Naturally the gentlemen would not wish to dine alone. One evening the chief purser walked into the first-class dining-room and noticed Anthony Quinn sitting at his table with a rather attractive young lady who had not been there the night before. He realized that she had 'come up' to dine and was not a first-class passenger. 'Good Heavens,' he said, 'that young lady is not one of ours!' He immediately called over the restaurant manager, who confirmed his suspicion. The problem was discussed and it was decided to let the matter rest rather than interrupt the meal, but the manager must refuse to allow the lady into the restaurant the following evening. The next night the manager saw Anthony Quinn approaching the dining-room entrance with the same girl on his arm. He drew himself up, took a deep breath and said, 'Excuse me, Mr Quinn sir . . .' and then suddenly visualized the actor in his tough film roles as his tall frame towered over him. All at once his courage failed and when Anthony Quinn replied, 'Yes Oscar, what were you going to say?' Oscar Bassam mumbled, 'Nothing sir, this way, follow me.' When he got back to the door, the chief purser said, 'Well, did you tell him, did you tell him?' 'Er, no,' replied Oscar, 'I decided that it was the chief purser's job.'

IF A PASSENGER in first class wished to entertain a guest from tourist or cabin class to dinner, he or she would have to get permission, and this could be a lengthy process. The final decision rested with the chief steward. Even with permission many first-class passengers would, not unreasonably, object. A classless society did not exist on board the two Queens.

In the very early days on board the bulk of the printing work was done ashore. All photographs taken were displayed on the boards and orders were taken by the shop-assistants. These orders were then passed on to the office in Southampton, where a team of girls printed them up and posted them off to all corners of the world. The post office sent a van each week, usually on a Wednesday, to collect as many as four sacks of mail. All the addresses were hand written and sorted into countries of destination and franked by hand, with the sea-mail rate of twopence-halfpenny. It is quite remarkable that during the many years the system operated only a minute percentage of orders went missing, and those that did were returned to the office in Southampton where they were filed away in the hope that someone might eventually claim them. One such returned order contained photographs of Liberace. He had specially requested that they be taken on board and had paid for them in advance, as was the practice. The completed order was sent out on time to his home address in America, where strangely, it was refused. The package was returned several times unopened, after many repeated attempts to deliver it. This mystified everyone at the office who were anxious to ensure that Liberace received his photographs. To this day they have never been claimed.

When the duty photographer had finished his embarkation shots on the pier in Cherbourg he would take advantage of being ashore and, taking his camera bag, would proceed to the nearest shop just across from the quayside. As crew were not allowed to purchase liquor on board or bring it with them, they took the opportunity to squeeze a couple of bottles of brandy into the camera bag, and by extending the bellows of the telephoto lens to its maximum length, could fill the void with an ample supply of Gauloise cigarettes. These luxuries could be enjoyed in the darkroom during the crossing to New York where further replenishments were acquired for the return trip.

The flash batteries were charged up overnight in the engine room, for, being inflammable they were not allowed to be charged in the darkroom. Even when fully discharged they still packed a punch, as one photographer found out. He had a surgical metal plate

Liberace photographed while dining in the Verandah Grill on board the *Queen Mary*.

fixed in his head as the result of a war injury and when he accidentally touched the contact plates on his flash battery he received a massive bolt from the residual power which sent him flying backwards across the darkroom and deposited him in a heap on the deck. Luckily, he survived, but it was a lesson well learnt.

One of the great difficulties of being a photographer at sea is to carry out the job without causing any inconvenience, offence, or interference with passengers' enjoyment of the trip. A certain amount of tact is needed, and in some situations a little humour. A difficult situation arose in a particularly attractive Caribbean port when passengers had been prevented from disembarking for several hours due to an administrative hitch. Since they were only in the port for a day they were understandably anxious to get ashore. This situation meant that there was little chance of stopping each passenger at the foot of the gangway for the customary 'view' shot. One photographer attempted to amuse the disgruntled passengers at the head of the queue by telling jokes and acting the fool, this was greatly appreciated and they obliged by posing for the camera. However, those further down the queue had had enough and there was a great surge forward. The photographer realized that his only chance was one enormous group shot so he raced down to the end of the pier to get ahead of the rush. He had to load new film as he ran and, looking over his shoulder, shouted to his colleague to organize the crowd into a group. As he turned to face the passengers he shouted 'Fine, great, thanks everyone, I can get you all in one picture . . . HOLD IT . . . HOLD IT . . .' He took one pace backwards and promptly fell off the end of the pier. Everyone raced to the edge and looked down, there he was, surfacing in a froth of bubbles, rising straight up out of the water, camera held high with a

silly grin on his face. Everyone roared with laughter and as he was hauled dripping wet from the sea he was deafened by the applause, some passengers believing he had performed the stunt deliberately. While he had been wallowing in the water, the other photographer had taken a picture of his demise, and that, together with the group shot, which was finally taken, proved to be the best sellers of the trip.

When photographs of the travelling celebrities were taken on board they were displayed in the usual way alongside pictures of other passengers, on the specially prepared dry-mounting boards. This system of display resulted in the theft of some of the celebrity pictures; so many disappeared that it was necessary to score the face of the photographs in order to deter the thieves. Even this measure did not dissuade the ardent larcenist, and eventually pictures of movie stars and royalty were not displayed in the sales areas. On one occasion a regular passenger on the Queens repeatedly 'removed' his personal photograph from the display. The chief photographer, noticing that the same 'family' went missing each day, left a note in the space saying 'Dear Mr . . . . , if you are so anxious to obtain a free photograph of yourself, please call by the darkroom and I will give you a copy, rather than have you mess up my display boards.' This seemed to have the desired effect and the thieving ceased.

Deck shots taken on leaving New York, and when the two Queens converged in mid Atlantic, were always popular and sold very well. The problem was trying to race along the deck taking as many pictures as possible before 'the view' vanished. As the ship gathered steam on her way back down the Hudson to the open sea, the backdrop of one of the most spectacular skylines in the world provided the perfect setting. If the weather was fine the most glorious

The Manhattan skyline provided many a backdrop for
amateur photographers on board.

sunsets would reflect in the many thousands of panes
of glass, and the glow from these reflections would
provide a form of natural back-lighting which gave the
photographs a luminous quality. There is nothing to
compare with sailing on one of the great Cunard liners
past the Manhattan skyline on a summer's evening.

In 1989, Ocean Pictures still carries on the great
tradition of photography at sea. This year celebrates
the sixtieth anniversary of the founding of the
company, and the same number of years in association
with Cunard Line Ltd. In these days of cut-throat

competition, intense rivalry and frequent take-over bids, this is an impressive record. The combination of traditional values and the use of the latest and most advanced photographic technology has been the backbone of a tried and tested operating policy.

With the implementation of highly efficient, computer controlled 'mini-labs', record development and processing speeds are now possible. Three years ago Ocean Pictures fitted out the *QE2* darkroom with the very latest computerized machine. This high-speed processor enables a colour print to be produced in forty-eight minutes. The entire process is done on one machine, eliminating the need to handle films several times, as is still necessary with conventional processing procedures.

As photography is an ever-changing medium, with more and more highly sophisticated machinery, keeping up with these technological advancements requires enormous capital outlay. Many of these amazing machines are likely to cost in excess of £100,000, so equipping each ship is a very expensive business. Despite these rocketing overheads, the price of a photograph on board has not risen correspondingly, therefore the potential for profit is not what it used to be. Small concessionaire companies are finding it increasingly more difficult to balance the books, especially when striving for perfection and a first-class service.

However, apart from the internal logistics of running a photographic company, the emphasis on the cruise-ship industry has changed dramatically. With the passenger figures on the North Atlantic having diminished over the years, the accent is now on the cruising/leisure market. This luxury end of the business has been enjoying a commercial boom since the sixties, and cruises are now available through various 'package deals', thus opening up a wider passenger market to the delights of tropical cruising. American cruise passengers dominate the market and patronize most international shipping lines, with one or two home-based companies taking the lion's share. Sadly, the threat of terrorist attack has seriously affected the cruise market in the Mediterranean and fewer American passengers are now prepared to fly to, and sail out of, 'high risk' ports. This has caused many companies to rethink their cruise schedules, and in many cases, pull out of the Mediterranean altogether. The result has been a blessing in disguise for other ports, especially home-based American ports like Miami, Los Angeles and the US Virgin Islands. The majority of shipping lines are now based on the eastern side of the Atlantic and more and more associated companies are following suit.

*T*HE *QUEEN MARY* DOCKED in Southampton on one sunny Saturday in June and the captain disembarked for a few hours to visit his wife at their home on the outskirts of town. As he climbed on to his modest pushbike and began pedalling home he was unaware of much grander goings on, only a very few miles distant from his own charted path. A wedding was taking place. A magnificent and lavish reception had been laid on for guests who had been flown across from America on a specially chartered plane. This was a very special wedding, it was not every day that the son of a chief barkeeper on one ship married the daugher of a chief barkeeper on another!

Gone are the days when the English port of South-ampton saw eleven or twelve ships a week sail in and out. The *QE2* is the last bastion of a greater age and she visits Southampton regularly throughout the

South Western House in Canute Road, Southampton, the headquarters for Cunard Line in England. It is situated opposite the main dock gates and was originally a grand railway hotel. Passengers arrived regularly on the boat-train and often stayed here the night before embarking.

summer on her transatlantic crossing schedule. The last great Queen is now very lonely in her home port. Ocean Terminal, one of the most famous landmarks in the port of Southampton, was razed to the ground two years ago. A magnificent example of Art Deco architecture was lost for ever, despite providing perhaps the perfect location for a much needed local maritime museum. The building itself was a monument to the great age of transatlantic liners, as memories of the boat train, luggage hall and the famous curved bar on the first floor, provided the perfect setting for passengers departing and arriving. Ocean Terminal was the gateway to England for innumerable transatlantic passengers and its loss is mourned by many.

Ocean Pictures, however, has not moved. The present office has been the head-quarters for the last forty years, and for twenty years before that the company was based around the corner in Oxford Avenue. Although tradition is important, it may prove necessary for the company to follow the trend and establish an overseas office. In today's highly competitive market flexibility is the key to survival. If Casimir Watkins were alive today he would definitely approve.

PART 2

CUNARD

A Brief History

Cunard

A Brief History

———————————— ☆ ————————————

*I*N 1880 THE CUNARD STEAMSHIP COMPANY was formed by Samuel Cunard. Since the early 1840s he had established an impressive record by winning lucrative contracts and gradually building and expanding the business. The company was originally known as 'The North American Steam Packet Company', the main bulk of the business being a mailship service to and from New York. As the company's reputation grew the speed and efficiency of this service attracted fare-paying passengers, and over the years Samuel Cunard's obsessive concern for safety won the Cunard Line increasing numbers of transatlantic travellers. Impressed by his record of no losses at sea, many passengers sailed with Cunard in preference to other lines, trusting in the Cunard company motto 'Speed, Comfort and Safety'. His concern for safety paid off handsomely in the days when disasters at sea were fairly commonplace, these were often due to incompetence or unnecessary risk-taking by the more unscrupulous shipping companies. The senior officers and masters of Cunard Line were instructed to follow a special code of practice, namely, 'no racing, rivalry or risk-taking'. This policy proved to be the foundation of the company's early success.

Over the years, the company changed the emphasis of its business. More passengers were carried and, although the mail was still faithfully delivered, the design of the transatlantic liner was altered considerably. In order to meet the challenge of increasingly cut-throat competition from rival lines, Cunard's policy was to offer passengers previously unattained luxury on board its liners. During the First World War merchant shipping suffered great losses and many passenger liners were sacrificed in the line of duty. As a result, there followed several years of intense activity in the boat-building yards as major replacement projects were undertaken. Samuel Cunard's ultimate ambition was to offer a two-ship service, back to back, across the Atlantic from Southampton to New York, following in the wake of those impressive giants of the sea, the *Aquitania*, *Mauretania* and *Berengaria*. And so, in 1930, the company's most ambitious project to date began as work started on the construction of a massive hull, number 534, and the keel of the *Queen Mary* was laid in John Brown's shipyard.

Unfortunately, soon after the project got underway it became clear that the depression was beginning to bite. The work on the hull was forced to a standstill after only one year – everyone involved in the project was bitterly disappointed. Eventually, after much

Cunard Line posters
from the years before
the Great War.

negotiation and bitter wrangling a deal was struck with the government, which stepped in after nearly three years of inactivity. Construction work restarted after the injection of a sizeable government subsidy. It was at this time, and as a condition of the government's support, that Cunard merged with the White Star Line, which was also experiencing financial difficulties. In theory, the merger would strengthen both companies and restore commercial stability. The company was relaunched with a new composite name – the Cunard White Star Line.

The *Queen Mary* was launched by the Queen, her namesake, in September 1934, and she came into service in 1936. The *Queen Mary* quickly established a reputation as the most glamorous liner afloat; she is affectionately remembered by many passengers and crew as the most loved and most luxurious of the two Queens. In the same year of her launch plans for the second ship were already well advanced. She was completed in record time; the speed and efficiency of the project ensured that the *Queen Elizabeth* was launched on schedule, in 1938. The timing was rather unfortunate. The political climate in Europe worsened and she was abandoned temporarily in an unfinished state. The John Brown Shipyard was put to more pressing projects of a military nature.

The *Queen Elizabeth* and her sister ship the *Queen Mary* both earned their spurs during the Second World War, providing a valuable contribution by transporting thousands of troops in the Indian Ocean and across the Atlantic. And so, despite having been officially launched several years earlier, the *Queen Elizabeth* did not begin her commercial service until 1946, when Samuel Cunard's ultimate dream was finally realized. The two Queens dominated the North Atlantic providing an efficient service for nearly thirty years.

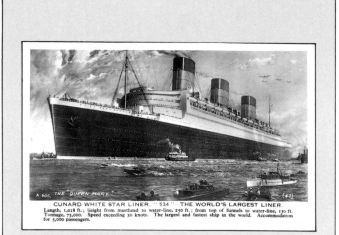

CUNARD WHITE STAR LINER. "534" THE WORLD'S LARGEST LINER.
Length, 1,018 ft.; height from masthead to water-line, 250 ft.; from top of funnels to water-line, 130 ft. Tonnage, 75,000. Speed exceeding 30 knots. The largest and fastest ship in the world. Accommodation for 5,000 passengers.

A FAMOUS STORY about the final choice of name for hull number 534 involved a misunderstanding between the Cunard chairman and King George V. It is said that when the chairman of Cunard consulted the royal household on the selection of a suitable name for the ship, popular consensus at the time was that she should be named 'Queen Victoria'. When Sir Percy Bates requested permission to name the ship after England's most illustrious Queen, he was somewhat taken aback when the King replied that his wife would be absolutely delighted. There was one other problem, however, in that certain wheels had already been put in motion because the involvement of the King was thought to be no more than a courteous formality. The fact that the new ship was now to be called *Queen Mary*, meant that thousands of items of crockery and porcelain had to be destroyed. Cunard had already given orders to various porcelain factories and most of the work had been completed with the finished china bearing the company logo and 'Queen Victoria'.

During this time they both carried passengers of prestige and international importance, as well as transporting many immigrants and refugees to a new life in America. The Blue Riband was perhaps the most coveted and prestigious prize for all transatlantic liners. This trophy was both won and lost many times, and competition was rife. The *Queen Mary* proudly held the record for twelve consecutive years, despite strong competition from her old rival, the *Normandie*. Cunard recognized the value of the Blue Riband as an effective marketing tool and sanctioned the contest.

AFTER ONLY A FEW MONTHS in service the *Queen Mary* captured the Blue Riband from her French rival the *Normandie*. She won this most coveted award by crossing the Atlantic in only three days, twenty-three hours and fifty-seven minutes. This was the official time recorded between the Ambrose Lightship to Bishop's Rock on the western coast of England. Her average speed was 30.63 knots, which is approximately thirty-five miles per hour. She had already completed a record-breaking westbound crossing from Southampton to New York in four days and twenty-seven minutes, beating the *Normandie* by well over two and a half hours. The combined east and westbound record times were sufficient to claim the Blue Riband for Cunard. Although the record was lost the following year to the *Normandie*, the *Queen Mary* broke yet another record in August 1938 when she crossed to England in three days, twenty-one hours and forty-eight minutes and Cunard once more claimed the prestigious trophy. The *Queen Mary* then held the record for fourteen consecutive years, until 1952, when the SS *United States* took the prize.

Left
The Restaurant, RMS *Queen Mary*.

Below
The Promenade Deck, RMS *Queen Elizabeth*.

Left
The Smoking Room, RMS *Queen Mary*.

There was widespread interest in the interior decoration of the *Queen Mary*. The ship received unprecedented publicity regarding the immense scope and variety of decorative finishes that graced her interior. Priceless works of art by many prominent contemporary artists and the most exquisite and rare woods were used in unusual and innovative ways – decorating the walls, as pieces of sculpture and inlaid with great precision to create masterpieces of marquetry. Paintings on canvas, hide and, unusually, silver, could be found throughout the ship. There were sculptures in rare woods and metals, bas reliefs, applied carvings and many novel forms of decorative glass. One of the most striking features of the *Queen Mary*'s decor was the extensive use of rare woods and veneers. No fewer than fifty-six varieties of wood were used, including such unusual specimens as pearwood, Japanese ash, quilted maple, tiger oak burr, zebrano, figured teak, bird's eye maple and Swedish birch. Such was the effect of the woods used in the *Queen Mary* that one is bound to lament the lack of colour photography on board. But even in black and white one can still appreciate the quality and richness of her interior design. Nothing can compare with seeing all these beautiful interiors at first hand, and not even advanced photographic techniques can reproduce the smell of waxed and polished woods. As a backdrop, these splendid rooms made ideal locations for many of the photographs taken on board. Some of the pictures in this book show tantalizing glimpses of a wide variety of the exquisite designs and works of art that adorned the *Queen Mary*.

THE *QUEEN MARY* BOASTED a magnificent carpet in the main lounge. It was handwoven, with silks and exquisite embroidery, and was absolutely priceless. It had been in position since the maiden voyage and was a masterpiece of creation, unique in design and a prime example of its kind. Several men arrived on board one day when the ship was docked and again offered official looking documentation authorizing its removal for cleaning. It was most carefully packed and rolled up and ceremoniously carried off the ship, never to be seen again.

ANOTHER OCCASION, on board the *Franconia*, saw the permanent removal of a white baby grand Steinway piano. Two men arrived, appropriately dressed, complete with a signed chit from the second steward, which gave them permission to remove the piano and take it ashore for retuning and repairing. As everything appeared to be in order the wine waiter, who happened to be passing through the room at the time, gave them the go-ahead to remove it. The men had the cheek to ask two waiters for assistance to carry it off the ship. They, of course, were totally unaware that they were accomplices to a major theft. It has never been seen since.

In many of the staterooms the fabrics were chosen to complement the woods used, and in some cases cloths were specially woven to imitate the grains and patinas of specific veneers. Each cabin or suite was decorated in a unique style; many passengers would request the same cabin each time they travelled – to many it felt like 'coming home' to a favourite room. Even the tourist-class areas were decorated with rare timbers, creating standards of luxury that were the envy of other passenger liners.

The *Queen Mary* offered the ultimate in ocean-going luxury, not only expressed in physical comfort and visual splendour, but in gastronomic excellence.

Dining on board was a mouth-watering experience. Cuisine unsurpassed in quality and variety was served smartly and efficiently amid exquisite surroundings. Each restaurant afforded varying degrees of exclusivity and privacy. Many stars and celebrities preferred to eat in the relative seclusion of the Verandah Grill, while others deliberately sought a more publicly prominent table reservation in the main first-class restaurant. Some never surfaced at all, choosing to dine in the total privacy of their own suites. The Verandah Grill featured on both the *Queen Mary* and the *Queen Elizabeth*. It catered exclusively for first-class passengers who sought to avoid the inevitable public attention in the main first-class restaurant. At night, after the evening fare had been ritually devoured, the tables were rearranged and a dance floor raised. A band would take up position and the Verandah Grill became a night club, with entertainment often continuing into the small hours of the morning. The rich and famous would dance amid their own glamorous company in this magnificent room, cooled by the ocean breeze on warm summer nights, which wafted in through fourteen distinctively elongated windows. Each was framed by heavy hand-stitched curtains, made from rich silk velvet and hand embroidered with glittering star motifs that sparkled as they caught the light.

WHILE ENJOYING THE INTERVALS between courses, and when starved of a new arrival into the dining-room down the grand staircase, or bored with the latest high-society gossip, passengers could feast their eyes on the sumptuous decor that surrounded them. The great transatlantic liners were famous for their opulence. Connoisseurs of fine art and stylish decor could appreciate the exquisite paintings and fabrics, the antique furniture, fine porcelain and sculptures that adorned every public room on the ship. The restaurants were no exception. This was the great attraction: a combination of glamour, culture and culinary delights, in addition to the obvious stimulation of rubbing shoulders with royalty, celebrated entrepreneurs and film stars. Unfortunately, connoisseurs were not the only ones to appreciate the wealth of material splendours on board. On several occasions, *objets d'art* and other items of value went permanently missing. On one occasion, on board the *Queen Mary*, the captain arrived at his table for dinner, only to discover that the impressive centre-piece, a beautiful sculpted silver rose bowl, was missing. An immediate and extensive search of the ship was launched, to no avail. An unfortunate crew member was blamed although his guilt was never proved, and despite a rigorous 'spring clean' of all corners of the vessel, no rose bowl came to light. Some months later, the New York police discovered it for sale in a downtown antique shop.

After nights of revelry and gourmet feasting, the morning brought forth many bleary eyed passengers to the open deck. Some, to take in fresh air, while the more energetic walkers braced themselves for a routine eight times round the deck, thus covering the ship's measured mile. The Duke and Duchess of Windsor attempted the ship's mile each time they travelled, not only for their own benefit, but in order to exercise their dogs who often accompanied them on voyages.

When the construction of the *Queen Elizabeth* was still at the visual conception stage, a company architect was dispatched on an 'undercover' mission to acquire one or two design ideas which had revolutionized the *Normandie*. He travelled incognito, and was very impressed with what he saw. Her innovative interiors

THE MAGNIFICENT CARPET in the Verandah Grill on the *Queen Mary* was one hundred per cent wool and jet black in colour. When it was first fitted there was uproar as some people considered the colour to be most unsuitable and impractical. However, because of its notoriety, it became a good talking point for first-time visitors to the Grill restaurant. It proved to be an excellent choice and graced the dining-room floor for many years.

PASSENGERS HAD THE OPTION of eating in the first-class restaurant, subject to their cabin status, or paying a supplement of ten shillings per meal to eat in the Verandah Grill. The surcharge did little to dissuade those from selecting the second option; bookings were made many months in advance, and in some cases passengers deferred their travel date to ensure a seat in the Grill.

☆

ON THE *QUEEN MARY* it was customary for the restaurant manager to do his grand tour of the restaurant on the last night of the voyage. This was a very important and necessary exercise as far as he was concerned as the number of satisfied passengers each trip had a direct effect on the size of tip he could expect later in the evening. Unfortunately for him, the *Queen Mary*'s first-class restaurant had a door at each end of the room; it was therefore impossible to be on duty at both doors simultaneously. He often found himself tied up at one exit engaged in conversation while out of the corner of his eye he could see potential gratuities disappearing rapidly out of the other door. This scenario was the cause of much amusement to one particular chef who regularly watched the fiasco from the door to the kitchens. The manager would often sprint from one end of the room to the other in a frantic attempt to say a personal 'farewell' to as many distinguished guests as possible. The trick was to appear casual and in control but there were times when this was anything but the case. When the *Queen Elizabeth* was built a few years later, it was said that the same restaurant manager put in a special request for one door only into the first-class dining-room. The final design revealed just one main door into the main restaurant.

OSCAR BASSAM, the Verandah Grill manager, not only ran the restaurant extremely efficiently, but turned his hand to concocting delicious desserts in a matter of minutes. He is remembered with great affection by many of the stars who travelled regularly and ate in the Grill. Not least, Bette Davis who, no matter which restaurant she patronized, would send for Oscar to create his most famous dessert, crêpes suzettes. Every time she travelled she would make a point of having at least one of Oscar's specialities.

☆

THE MENUS IN THE GOLDEN DAYS offered an enormous selection of dishes, including a wide variety of delicacies, exotic meats and preserves. The main problem was keeping produce fresh and in prime condition. Inevitably fish featured regularly on the daily menu during the first couple of days of the voyage so that it was served while still at the peak of freshness. The same policy applied to the most perishable of foods and in this way a great variety of culinary delights were available to an appreciative clientele.

☆

THE VERANDAH GRILL BAR was a famous meeting place for many guests. Its location, tucked just inside the door of the Verandah Grill, offered the privacy and seclusion not otherwise found in the larger social areas on board. The Grill Bar had a club-like intimacy, which suited many who sought peace and quiet. It became a popular venue as the first port of call on many a pleasant evening.

THE VERANDAH GRILL restaurant had the most beautiful hand-made sets of curtains. They were very heavy, made from an exquisite silk brocade, and embroidered with huge stars which sparkled at night.

The Verandah Grill, RMS *Queen Mary*.

and exterior lines had been a major contributory factor in her many successful attempts to win the Blue Riband. As a result of this unofficial foray, a large number of the *Normandie*'s finer design details were the source of inspiration for many of the *Queen Elizabeth*'s graceful and practical interiors. The *Queen Elizabeth* was a bigger ship than the *Queen Mary*. She was twelve feet longer and had more accommodation and recreational deck space. The Verandah Grill on the *Queen Mary* seated about eighty, whereas the same restaurant on the *Queen Elizabeth* had an extended capacity and could comfortably accommodate about one hundred and twenty covers. The *Elizabeth* had only two funnels, compared with the *Mary*'s three, thus creating a much larger and clearer area on the top deck, with many of the offending air vents relocated or removed altogether. This gave passengers more freedom of movement and recreational space, allowing easier access to the upper decks.

Before the outbreak of war, there was much advance publicity about the new sister ship and her imminent construction. Even before the keel had been laid the first bookings for her maiden voyage came flooding in, although she was not scheduled to sail for at least three years and because of the war, she did not sail on her first commercial voyage for almost eight years. The *Queen Elizabeth* was launched from the John Brown Shipyard on the Clyde by the Queen, again her namesake, on 27th September 1938. It was formally announced that she would make her maiden voyage in April 1940. However, the outbreak of the Second World War resulted in a change of plan; the *Queen Elizabeth* was now a prime enemy target and it became imperative for her to find a safe berth. Although she carried no weaponry, her main defence against attack was her speed and manoeuvrability and this ensured her safety. The true destination of the *Queen Elizabeth*'s first voyage was a well-kept secret. She arrived at Pier 90 in New York safely and without incident, after a daring voyage across the Atlantic.

ON BOTH THE *QUEEN MARY* and the *Queen Elizabeth* the policy of segregation between the classes was rigorously upheld. The most effective method of keeping passengers apart was strategically placed gates positioned at intervals throughout the open deck, and below; thick braided decorative ropes were used to define the 'no-go' areas for those not in first-class accommodation. Although no ship's officers manned the posts, it was unheard of for anyone to trespass across the clearly defined boundaries. Everyone knew their place and the odd one or two who tried it on were quickly spotted by the ever vigilant duty officers. Depending on the

---

RMS QUEEN ELIZABETH—Basic Facts

Gross tonnage: 83,673
Overall length: 1,031 feet
Width: 118 feet
Draft: 38 feet
Engines: steam turbines with quadruple screws

Speed: average 28.5 knots
Capacity: 823 first class; 662 cabin class; 798 tourist class
Built: John Brown's Shipyard, Clydebank, Scotland
Caught fire and capsized in Hong Kong harbour, 9th January 1972

number of first-class passengers carried on each voyage, these barriers would be moved along the upper decks. The amount of space taken up by the first-class sections on board was staggering in comparison with cabin and tourist class. Well over half the allocated passenger space was given over to first class, with the remaining less attractive deck locations divided between the other sections. Cabin class was situated aft, first class taking up a considerable amount of space amidships, and tourist class was always forward. In pitching seas, with no stabilizers, the least comfortable place to ride the storm was the section behind the bows. Tourist-class passengers were constantly buffeted and bumped as the liners heaved and cork-screwed a channel through the waves. In really bad weather the bows would rise up and hang, apparently motionless, over the edge of an enormous swell of water and then suddenly crash down into the trough of the wave with tremendous speed, hitting the water with frightening force. It would sound to the unitiated like an explosion and it was not uncommon to experience the effects of 'G' force afterwards as the ship shuddered and wallowed before finding her own natural stability. Some would argue that it was worse to be situated over the propellers in the aft section of the ship. Here one not only had to contend with the effects of stormy weather, but the constant vibration from the engine room below. Even in fine weather it was impossible to risk leaving any moveable objects unattended in the cabin. Placing a glass of water on the bedside table before retiring was a mistake which caught many unseasoned travellers unawares.

The *Queen Elizabeth* slipped into New York painted a dreary battleship grey, with many of her lifeboats missing and much work still to be carried out on her interior. Happily, her appearance did not detract from the welcome she received in New York, as the news of her arrival had been leaked when a TWA plane spotted the liner a few miles off the coast in New York Bay. Thousands of people turned out to welcome her as she steamed up the Hudson, and for the first time she berthed alongside her sister ship, the *Queen Mary*. After a period of several months lying idle both ships were recruited by the navy to serve as troop ships for the duration of the war.

The decor on the *Queen Elizabeth* varied greatly from that of her companion ship, the *Queen Mary*. Although a large quantity of wood was put to decorative use, the overall effect was much lighter and brighter. The most striking difference was the addition of two garden lounges, situated on promenade deck. These beautiful new areas provided passengers with an 'open air' effect whilst being protected from the unpredictable elements of the Atlantic. They were filled with an exotic array of foliage and this, in addition to all the fresh flowers which decorated the ship, kept a full-time gardener busy.

Many of the designers who had contributed to the interiors of the *Queen Mary* were rehired to assist with creating a new look for the *Queen Elizabeth*. The most obvious difference was that a greater variety of materials were used in the design of her interiors. A large quantity of leather was put to good effect in the panelling of walls and many brass and copper engravings and glass sculptures graced her public rooms. The most striking individual decoration on the *Queen Elizabeth* was a huge marquetry panel depicting Chaucer's Canterbury pilgrims. The design incorporated nearly seventy different types of wood, many from England including a veneer taken from a virginia

The Queen Mother is introduced to the *Queen Mary*'s senior officers.

*H*ER MAJESTY, THE QUEEN MOTHER, made many visits to the Queens, and on occasion travelled on board. For one of the early trips a suite had been completely stripped and lavishly re-designed at enormous expense in honour of the occasion. The designer of this beautiful new suite of rooms anxiously stood on the gangway with other company dignitaries awaiting her arrival. He had created a peaceful and tranquil effect by using rich tones and shades of green. While waiting for Her Majesty to arrive he began chatting to one of her aides who had come aboard early and had just inspected her quarters. On discovering that he was talking to the designer, the aide confided that he was afraid that Her Majesty may wish to be given another suite of rooms as she was extremely superstitious and did not like the colour green.

Despite the designer's fears the Queen Mother was delighted with the accommodation and her apparent aversion to the colour green was never mentioned.

*W*HEN THE QUEEN MOTHER travelled on board the *Queen Mary*, she dined in the Verandah Grill and, although she always stayed in her suite for breakfast and lunch, it was customary for her to entertain selected guests at her table in the evenings. Her Majesty's order for dinner would always be given in advance, and the head chef in the Verandah Grill kitchen would be responsible for ensuring that her food was perfectly cooked and presented. This was quite a task, as stove space was rather limited in the small cooking area, so a large quantity of food was cooked and prepared several decks below in another kitchen. It was therefore extremely difficult to co-ordinate the food being cooked upstairs with the food coming up on a dumb waiter from below. A commendable amount of precision and skill was needed to ensure that a perfectly cooked meal was served on time and at the peak of freshness from the oven. Chef John Bainbridge remembers one occasion when Her Majesty had ordered a sirloin of beef and to play safe he had arranged for two to be cooked simultaneously just in case one did not meet with his own personal standards. At the last minute the two sirloins were delivered at top speed up through the ship on the dumb waiter from below and as John cut them both he was horrified to find that neither one was acceptable. A new joint of beef was cooked and fresh vegetables were prepared. After the meal Her Majesty sent congratulations and had been unaware of the lengthy delay between courses.

creeper grown at Hampton Court Palace which was said to be a 120 years old.

Another interesting design feature was the use of timber salvaged from the piles driven under the original Waterloo Bridge in 1911. These handsome timbers were appropriately employed in the panelling of the captain's cabin, where the fine grain was shown to its best advantage after years of buffing by the tidal waters of the Thames. The position of the captain's cabin was beneath the bridge, so this was considered to be a most apt location for the rescued wood.

Both ships had enormous maps showing the relative daily positions of each vessel. The *Queen Elizabeth*'s version of the great transatlantic map was situated in the first-class smoking-room and formed the backdrop for many totes and auctions that were held during the crossings. A similar map was situated in the dining-saloon of the *Queen Mary*; this was a much larger version and its elevated position allowed passengers to follow the ship's course while enjoying their food.

*I*T IS INTERESTING to note that several forms of gambling were available on board, although in fairly innocuous forms, such as horse-racing, housey-housey, card games and the daily tote. All these events were extremely well attended, with many people happy to stand when seats were not available. The most popular was the daily tote. It was hard not to be drawn into this one, as the smoking-room was dominated by an enormous map of the North Atlantic showing the routes of both eastbound and westbound crossings, the main attraction being a hypnotic pair of red pulsating lights signifying the *Queen Mary* and *Queen Elizabeth* on ever converging paths as they crossed the Atlantic from opposite sides. As each mile was covered, the light moved correspondingly. The aim of the tote was to guess the number of miles covered each day, the more technical participants allowing for fluctuations in speed due to inclement weather conditions. Some regular travellers became quite adept at guessing correctly, and frequently the same competitor won the coveted prize. Gambling, in whatever form, has a guaranteed following, particularly from those who are a captive audience. Passengers on transatlantic voyages, with several days at sea at a stretch, are prime targets. Shipping companies have been quick to recognize the lucrative money-earning potential of gambling in all its forms. Many passenger ships now provide their own fully operational casinos, largely to counteract the lure of shore-side casinos in ports of call.

Bellboys stand at attention for an inspection on Sun Deck during the *Queen Mary*'s maiden voyage.

A SAD LOSS TO today's passenger ships are the bellboys. These young men always took pride in the job and in many ways were the envy of other members of the crew, not least because of their potential earning power. The boys on the door of each restaurant had the knack of turning on the charm and this ability to brighten the day of many an ageing dowager ensured a healthy money-box at the end of each voyage. It was not unknown for them to earn more in gratuities than the waiters, and as the doors were swung wide to admit a party of guests a 'Good evening, how charming madam looks tonight, and what a beautiful gown . . .' was enough to ensure a favourable response. Sincerity was not essential to the job.

The first commercial voyage of the *Queen Elizabeth* began on 16th October 1946. She sailed from Southampton under the command of Captain Sir James Bisset, Commodore of the Cunard Line. There was a glittering passenger list, including prominent politicians, royalty and famous actors and actresses. The Russian delegates to the United Nations, Vishinsky and Molotov, were on board and strict security was enforced. Because of the food shortages in England most of the provisions necessary for the voyage were imported from abroad, and for many passengers still suffering the effects of rationing, the menus offered on that first voyage must have appeared like manna from heaven. The ship's doctor was unusually busy on the maiden voyage, for many passengers delighting in the choice of marvellous food after the hardships of war fell ill from over-indulgence.

The other temptation on board, which had inspired many to book a passage, was revealed as huge queues formed outside the new shopping area. The luxuries displayed inside were eagerly sought by people who had grown used to the mundane selections at home. As soon as the doors opened a stampede of passengers burst into the well-stocked areas; as a result, after the ship's staff intervened, the shops were shut again until some semblance of order had been restored. The shops on board had a bumper trip, and in many cases sold out of some lines before the ship had reached the open sea.

The two great liners passed for the first time on the evening of 25th July 1947. As the *Queen Mary* approached the Nab Tower on her way up the solent, the *Queen Elizabeth* was beginning her eighteenth voyage to New York. The weekly express service which had been the dream of Samuel Cunard was finally operational: on the 31st July 1947 the *Queen Mary* sailed from Southampton and the next day the *Queen Elizabeth* sailed from New York. Their paths across the Atlantic were carefully planned so that they could pass within sight of each other, thus providing a point of interest for passengers on both ships. This marketing ploy was encouraged for many years, and its effect on both crew and passengers engendered a sense of patriotism and loyalty to the company.

Margaret Lockwood sitting in a quiet corner of the
Main Lounge, Promenade Deck.

Lionel Barrymore stands in the central thoroughfare of
the Main Lounge on Promenade Deck.

Noel Coward completely at home on the upper deck.

Marlene Dietrich holds on to her hat, on the Sports Deck.

Fred Perry, tennis hero, finds a temporary resting place.

Gracie Fields relaxes in the drawing-room
on Promenade Deck.

Gloria Swanson takes in some fresh air on the Boat Deck.

Fred Astaire on his way up to the top deck.

PHOTOGRAPH ON BOARD
R.M.S. "QUEEN MARY"

Douglas Fairbanks Jnr dances into the early hours on
the Verandah Grill dance floor.

Mary Pickford at the dressing table in her luxury suite.

Gary Cooper and his wife with an early
Cunard White Star lifebelt.

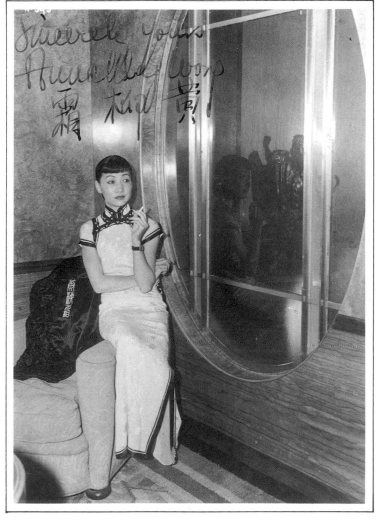

Anna May Wong enjoys the view from a quiet corner
of the Main Lounge.

Leslie Howard enjoying summer sunshine on the Boat Deck.

Johnny Weismuller, Tarzan, on the Sports Deck.

*D*OLORES DEL RIO, the popular actress, understandably attracted many suitors. Errol Flynn was an enthusiastic admirer and always said that he thought she was the most beautiful woman he had ever seen.

Lili Damita, Errol Flynn's wife on the Promenade Deck.

Dolores Del Rio exercises her bull terrier on the Promenade Deck.

Anna Neagle in her first-class suite.

Constance Bennett takes a stroll on deck
on the maiden voyage.

PART 3

THE WAR YEARS

1940–1945

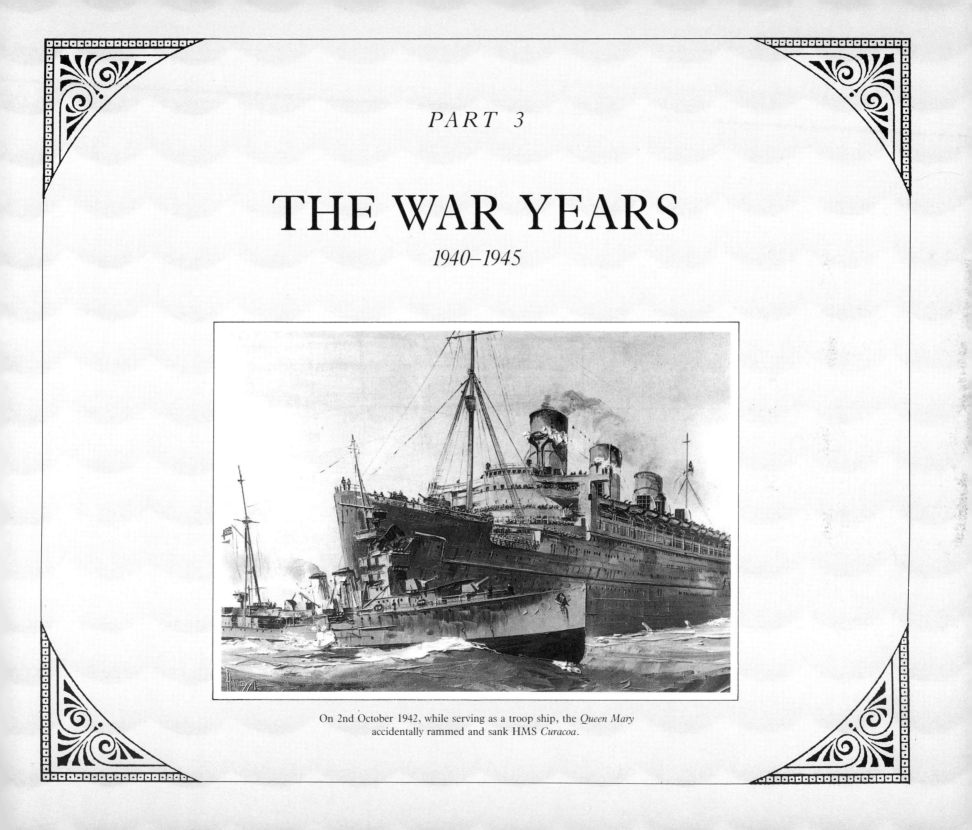

On 2nd October 1942, while serving as a troop ship, the *Queen Mary* accidentally rammed and sank HMS *Curacoa*.

The War Years

1940–1945

☆

*P*IER 90, NEW YORK, 7TH MARCH 1940. The magnificent new liner, *Queen Elizabeth* finally docked alongside her sister ship, *Queen Mary*, having made a successful dash across the Atlantic. The Nazis had been cleverly outwitted by Cunard, who had managed to keep the true destination of the ship a closely guarded secret. Publicly, no one knew of her intended route from John Brown's Shipyard, but false information was deliberately 'leaked' in the hope that the Germans would pick up the scent and follow a false trail. The fact that German Luftwaffe planes were reported circling over the English Channel at a time when the *Queen Elizabeth* was supposedly due to sail through *en route* to Southampton, is likely proof that the bait was taken.

Cunard, with the pride of its merchant fleet lying idle in New York, was faced with the problem of what to do with the two liners for the duration of the war. No one at that time had any idea how long the hostilities in Europe would last, nor how all encompassing the war would prove to be. One of the suggestions put forward was that the Queens should be converted into aircraft carriers, with capacity for planes and a large number of troops. The idea was thrown out because conversion costs would have been prohibitive and the work would take at least ten months to complete. Another unpopular suggestion, put forward by a politician, was to sell both ships to the United States.

After much discussion between government ministers and company officials, it was decided that the two liners could best serve the war effort by assuming the role of troop-carriers. As this would involve certain modifications to the ships' interiors, a suitable port had to be found so that work could begin. This refit could not take place in neutral America. Eight months after lying idle in New York, the *Queen Elizabeth* sailed for Singapore, and dry dock. Singapore was chosen in preference to Sydney (where refitting work on the *Queen Mary* was well underway) because it obviated the need to remove the ship's masts to negotiate Sydney Harbour Bridge.

The *Queen Elizabeth* did go to Australia in February 1941, and it was from Sydney that the two Queens first sailed together on 9th April 1941. Initially, both ships carried Australian troops to Suez for the campaign in the Middle East. In May 1941, an historical event occurred when both Queens travelled in convoy, unescorted, through the Red Sea from Aden to Suez. In December 1941 the Japanese attacked the American naval base at Pearl Harbour and America entered the

Obscured by smoke from the tugs, the *Queen Mary* arrives in Sydney Harbour.

war. It was essential to get large numbers of American troops quickly and efficiently to Australia and the two Queens were picked as the obvious and most suitable mode of transportation – being the fastest vessels afloat with the largest carrying capacity. With the Japanese advancing through Malaya towards the East Indies and the Philippines, considerable importance was placed on getting these essential support troops to a back-up

position in Australia and never before had the speed and efficiency of the *Queen Elizabeth* and the *Queen Mary* been so vital.

One of the great problems facing the two ships during the war was finding suitable locations *en route* for refuelling. As they had both been built specifically for the transatlantic service the taking on of fuel and provisions would have been done at the end of each

Left
Returning American troops receive a tumultuous
welcome as the *Queen Mary* docks in New York.

Above
Gambling on board the *Queen Mary* helped to relieve the
tedium for American troops *en route* for the front.

Left
The elegant public rooms were converted for troop-ship
duty; the Grand Salon became a huge mess hall.

crossing. The evasive and circuitous routes that of necessity were taken by the two liners during the war meant that in many cases the distance travelled exceeded their fuel carrying capacity and refuelling had to be performed secretly at sea. This procedure helped to protect the true position of the ship, but it was essential that the support vessel was in the right place at the right time – a large passenger liner was a prime target.

At the beginning of their troop-carrying service each of the Queens carried approximately 5,000 military personnel. As the demands became greater as the war dragged on both ships would individually carry as many as 13,000–15,000 troops – in some cases entire divisions were transported at any one time. With this many passengers on board eating and sleeping became a major operation. Special canvas bunkbeds which hung in tiers six at a time were erected wherever space permitted. A two-bedroomed stateroom could accommodate as many as forty soldiers at any one time, and there were at least two shifts a night! Feeding the troops was a continual process throughout the day, and involved consecutive shifts in the dining-rooms. It was impossible for the kitchens to provide three meals a day, so the daily menu was reduced to two meals per man per day. The Cunard kitchen crew were able to produce two hot meals per head per day from within the same kitchens, using the same facilities, that were normally deemed appropriate for 1,500 passengers: one tenth of the number they found themselves catering for on a regular basis throughout the two liners' war service!

ON BOARD THE *Queen Elizabeth* in the early days of 1942, while carrying out her duties as a troop ship, a British officer was approached on deck by a young American naval lieutenant. He asked the officer where he could go to get a drink, having already searched without success for a likely bar. The officer pointed out that as there were a large number of American servicemen travelling on this particular voyage it had been stipulated that the vessel be a 'dry' ship, in accordance with American military law. They continued to chat for a few minutes and he was such an engaging young man that the British officer took a risk and decided to invite him up to the wardroom for a drink. All the senior ship's officers were already in the wardroom enjoying their regular lunchtime pint of beer. When they arrived at the wardroom door, the officer realized that he did not know the young lieutenant's name and he was about to introduce him to his colleagues. You can imagine his surprise when the American replied 'My name is Douglas Fairbanks'.

TWO YEARS LATER the same officer was serving on board the *Aquitania*. They were alongside in New York when the chief officer ordered him down below to tally the registered mail. He dutifully went down to the mailroom where the master at arms told him that the registered mail had not yet arived. So rather than return empty handed he decided to stay below until the delivery came. Seeing a box in the corner covered with a tarpaulin he sat down on it to wait. The master at arms looked across at him and said 'Do you realize who you are sitting on?' The officer jumped up in surprise, and lifting the tarpaulin, saw to his horror that he had been sitting on a coffin. It contained the body of Annie Oakley, who was being taken home for burial in England.

ONE AMUSING EVENT occurred while the *Aquitania* was serving time as a troop-ship during the war. Following in the footsteps of her big sisters, the *Queen Mary* and *Queen Elizabeth*, she had spent the early part of the war ferrying troops from Australia to Egypt and the Middle East. As D-Day approached, she was called away from her routine work and received instructions to join forces with the Queens on the North Atlantic run, carrying United States servicemen to Europe. Prior to one particular crossing a large number of coloured American servicemen embarked with the rest of their regiment and spent a few hours familiarizing themselves with the ship that was to be their home for the next few days. After sailing, a number of the soldiers visited the general supplies shop on board and it soon became clear to the sales assistant that there was to be an unusually high demand for hair tonic on the voyage. This proved to be the case as, on the second day at sea on her way out from New York, the entire ship's stock of hair tonic ran out. Now, this was not exactly a major disaster, but to the shop manager on board, realizing that he was about to lose a large number of sales over the remaining three days of the voyage, it was pretty serious. Being an enterprising chap, he looked along the shelves in the store room and noticed an unnecessarily large supply of sun-tan oil – demand for this product was virtually zero on the North Atlantic in mid-winter. As sun-tan oil is alcohol based, he quickly realized its potential. All the labels were steamed off and within a few hours, a new supply of 'hair tonic' suddenly appeared on the shelves. This revolutionary new mixture proved to be an instant success and it obviously did an excellent job for when the ship docked in Southampton not one bottle remained on the shelves. The local shore-side office handling the ship's stores was amazed at the number of bottles of sun-tan oil that had been sold, it was a complete mystery, as the weather on the way across had been bleak and miserable.

As plans for the invasion of Europe began to take shape the **Queen Elizabeth** and *Queen Mary* went into service in the North Atlantic. The quality of materials and the standard of workmanship employed in the construction stages proved to be one of the major contributing factors in maintaining an impressive record for consistent speed and performance. These qualities had proved invaluable during the early war years and would come to play an even greater role in the North Atlantic where the threat of attack was far greater. The two Queens became prize targets for every U-boat commander and it was rumoured at the time that Hitler personally offered a substantial reward to any German officer, in the navy or the air force, who could sink one of the Queens. Never before had the words 'speed and safety,' the old Cunard motto, played such an important role as the two ships began their tour of duty in the cold and bleak North Atlantic.

Cruisers provided a protective escort when the *Queen Mary* and *Queen Elizabeth* entered U-boat-infested waters.

It was vital that the two ships never sailed the same route across the ocean, instead they would endeavour to outwit the enemy by steering a zig-zag course, changing direction erratically and as often as possible. It is quite remarkable that no one who travelled on the Queens during the war lost their lives. There was only one tragic incident, which occurred off the coast of Ireland on a westbound crossing in October 1942, which serves to mar their otherwise impeccable war service record. Travelling at top speed, and fully laden, the *Queen Mary* rammed and split in two an escort cruiser, HMS *Curacoa*. The warship was severely damaged and sank in a matter of minutes, resulting in massive loss of life – over three hundred and fifty dead and very few survivors. It must have been a very difficult decision for the captain of the *Queen Mary* but the threat of undetected U-boats was ever present and if he had followed his instincts and offered assistance he would have put more lives at risk.

DURING THE WAR YEARS, the two Queens carried many American soldiers to Europe. They were in and out of New York so much that some GIs began to think of the ships as their own. It was not until after the war that the families of the GIs travelled on the Queens in an attempt to relive the experiences of those interim years. They wanted to see the ship that 'Dad had travelled over to England on', and many would come on board and say to the officers, 'Hey, are you a Limey? What are you doing on an American ship?' Some of the relatives got very upset when they were politely told that the *Queen Mary* and the *Queen Elizabeth* were actually British ships and, in some cases, would only accept the truth when shown one of the historical brochures.

On another occasion, later that year, the Germans claimed that they had scored a direct hit on the *Queen Elizabeth*; it is true that several torpedos were fired, but fortunately none found its mark. There were many close shaves, and one or two reported near misses, for both ships over the next two years. But the *Queen Mary* and *Queen Elizabeth* continued to transport thousands of troops across to Europe quickly, efficiently and safely, although constantly exposed to danger.

DAME MYRA HESS, the concert pianist who entertained passengers on both ships, was created a Dame for her contribution to the war effort. She played to troops and civilians in venues both large and small and was greatly loved by all who heard her perform.

The return westbound voyages usually involved the transportation of the wounded and sick back from the front lines. Consequently large sections of the ship were designated hospital areas and nursing staff had to work under extremely difficult conditions in unfamiliar surroundings to care for the injured. The turkish bath became the X-ray room, and the dance salon was turned into an enormous ward; the hospital beds were positioned athwartships to prevent the wounded from falling out of bed when the ship rolled, which was most of the time as neither were fitted with stabilizers.

At the end of the war, both ships were decommissioned and sent to John Brown's Shipyard for refurbishment. For the *Queen Elizabeth* this meant commercial service at last. Furniture, china, works of art and linens, were brought out of store from all over the country. As many as 20,000 items of furniture and 9,000 items of linen and carpets were retrieved and gathered together for sorting in one enormous warehouse. The ships' hulls were once more revealed beneath the battleship grey camouflage paint, and the Cunard colours reappeared on the funnels and superstructure. The *Queen Elizabeth* went into commercial service for the first time in October 1946 and was joined by her sister ship the following summer. Both liners proved themselves to be the most popular and profitable ships offering a service across the North Atlantic. They continued to rule the waves for fifteen years until the industry declined at the beginning of the sixties. But few people today remember the role played by the two Cunard liners and their crews during the Second World War. Sir Winston Churchill acknowledged their valuable contribution when he said:

The world owes a debt to these two great ships that will not be easy to measure. Vital decisions depended upon their ability to continuously elude the enemy, and without their aid the final day of victory must unquestionably have been postponed.

Ronald Coleman and his wife Benita Hume, wave goodbye
to New York as the *Queen Mary* gathers speed
en route for Europe.

Actress Greer Garson, studying the ship's programme after checking into her suite.

Claude Raines, Alida 'Valli', Glen Ford and Lloyd Bridges meet up on the Sports Deck of the *Queen Mary* before sailing for England.

Anna Neagle and Michael Wilding talk to film director
Herbert Wilcox, and a Cunard chef in the Verandah Grill.

Virginia Mayo, Peggy Cummins and Michael O'Shea pose
with Peggy's mother on their way to dinner.

Sam Goldwyn, film director, stands before the magnificent
marble fireplace in the Main Lounge on the *Queen Mary*.

Joseph Rank, film magnate, and his wife walk the
measured mile along the Boat Deck.

Eric Von Stroheim, film director, takes in the scenery
from the Sports Deck.

Mr and Mrs Ernest Bevin.

WHEN MR GROMYKO was on board, the chef would go to great lengths to prepare authentic Russian food. After the first two evenings the manager enquired whether the food was satisfactory, as Mr Gromyko had not managed to conceal his disappointment. Being a true diplomat he had not wanted to draw attention to the fact that what he had been looking forward to was eating Western food. From then on he selected all his meals from the main menu. Mr Gromyko always gave generous gratuities, but he deliberately favoured the waiters and busboys, never the restaurant manager or head wine waiter, as he considered them to be capitalists. His socialist principals did not prevent him, or any of his entourage, from habitually travelling in first-class passenger cabins when crossing the Atlantic.

Mr Gromyko, the Russian Delegate, dines with a colleague in the first-class dining-room on the *Queen Mary*.

Actress Beatrice Lillie, Lady Peel, rests on the
Promenade Deck, *Queen Mary*.

Beatrice Lillie was a very popular passenger on board. As Lady Peel, she was a regular guest at the captain's table. One evening, she arrived about twenty minutes after the other guests had been seated and one rather pompous American lady was not very impressed. She complained rather loudly saying, 'Ladies should never arrive late for dinner', to which Beatrice Lillie replied, 'Lady Peel will arrive whenever she chooses, and is therefore never late.'

Somerset Maugham no doubt gathering material for his next
novel.

Mrs Roosevelt in her suite on the *Queen Elizabeth*.

Helen Keller, with travelling companions, in her suite on
the *Queen Elizabeth*.

Victor Mature catching the breeze on the
Boat Deck, *Queen Mary*.

Burt Lancaster with fellow actor Nick Crowat,
pictured in the Smoking Room, *Queen Elizabeth*.
They starred in many films together.

Max BEAR, the famous boxer, was seen to grab hold of an attractive young lady in the middle of a crowded public room on board and ask her loudly if she had ever been hugged by a bear before, because if she hadn't, she could now say she had.

Lee Savole, the boxer, checks the lifeboats on the Boat Deck.

Francis L Sullivan reports on a boxing tournament watched by eager crew and passenger enthusiasts.

Joe LEWIS, the world heavyweight boxing champion, while crossing to Europe with his entourage, sent a member of his party to seek out a snack from one of the kitchens. As it was between meals, a weary young chef was clearing up the kitchen when the young messenger stuck his head around the door. 'Can you get us a couple of apples Bud?', he enquired. The chef said 'No, I'm sorry Sir, I don't have any up here'. 'That's a real shame', he said, 'Joe would really like some fruit right now'. 'Joe who?' said the Chef. 'Why, Joe Lewis of course!' 'What! Joe Lewis? He can have *anything* he wants, just name it.' The chef dashed off to the cold store and was back with a whole basket of selected fruit.

Rex Harrison and Lilli Palmer seem delighted with
their stateroom.

Edward Underdown and Carole Landis stroll the upper decks
pre-sailing from Southampton.

*R*EX HARRISON AND LILLI PALMER were affectionately known on the Queens as 'Sexy Rexy
and Diamond Lil' because of his magnetic screen
presence and sparkling personality and her passion
for jewellery, expensive clothes and money. It was
widely reported at the time that Carole Landis was
pregnant with his child after a long and protracted
affair. Rex Harrison refused to divorce Lilli Palmer
and in a desperately dramatic gesture Carole Landis
committed suicide at the age of twenty-nine.

Edward Underdown and Carole Landis take their cues from
the directors during a pause in filming out on deck.

*H*ARVEY FIRESTONE and his wife were great friends with Rex Harrison and Lillie Palmer. They were regularly seen together socializing in the Verandah Grill late at night and often until the early hours of the morning. It was not unusual for some of these late-night owls to see in the dawn and, as party revellers with such impressive stamina, their staying power was often rewarded with an early breakfast of smoked salmon and scrambled eggs, washed down with a bottle of champagne. Travelling at sea affords one the memorable experience of witnessing magnificent sunrises and sunsets. There can be no better way to end an enjoyable evening than to sit in the Verandah Grill, with the windows flung wide to catch the early morning sea-breezes, with the eastern horizon announcing the imminent sunrise.

Filming on board is hazardous enough without the humorous
antics of Lou Costello.

Laurel and Hardy in a rare picture with their wives,
embark on a night out.

Jimmy 'Schnozzle' Durante, amuses delighted passengers on
the Boat Deck, *Queen Elizabeth*.

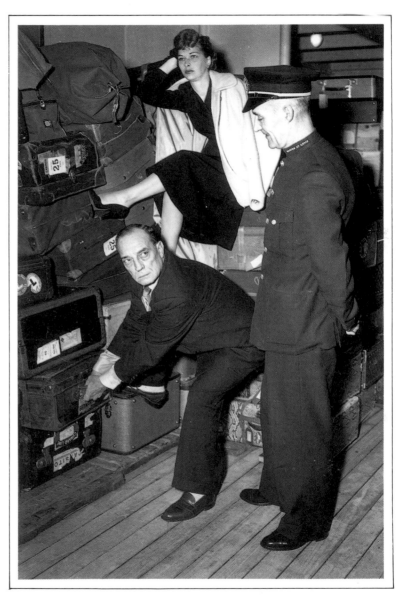

Buster Keaton with his wife and the master-at-arms, in comic
pose on the Promenade Deck of the *Queen Mary*.

The Duke and Duchess would often exercise their dogs along
the ship's measured mile.

O N MOST EVENINGS during the five-day crossing
the Duke of Windsor would take a walk around
the upper decks, long after the Duchess had retired
for the night. It became a routine. He enjoyed the
peace and solitude, puffing on his pipe, happy and
content with his own company. Towards the end
of his late-night stroll, he would often call in for a

chat with the night-watch officers on the bridge.
The Duke relished his visits to this inner sanctum
of the ship and was known to stay for as long as
half an hour, discussing navigation, the weather and
nautical topics of conversation. He showed a great
interest in how the ship was run and followed up
on incidents that occurred during the daily operation of the ship's itinerary. He was a popular visitor
and is affectionately remembered by the bridge
officers who spoke regularly with him on these
nocturnal visits.

Opposite
The Duke and Duchess of Windsor were frequent travellers
on board the two Cunard flagships.

*J*UST BEFORE ONE OF the first trips made by the Duke and Duchess of Windsor, the Duke's valet, Mr Campbell, gave instructions to the chief purser about the manner of address. He requested that Wallis be treated as royalty and be addressed as 'Your Highness' at all times. The Duchess appeared to dominate the Duke. She would frequently scold him in public for over-indulgence. On one occasion, at the end of dinner, she ordered the waiter to remove the second glass of brandy from the table, the Duke having ordered it a few minutes earlier. So great was her displeasure she rose abruptly, said goodnight to the assembled party, and announced, in front of a rather surprised Duke, that they were now retiring for the night. Nobody argued with Wallis!

Right
The Duke and Duchess give a press conference prior to departure.

David Niven and his wife Hjordis pose for the camera out on
deck.

Clark Gable chats to the purser on board the
Queen Mary.

Maurice Chevalier strolling along Promenade Deck, the
Queen Mary.

Rita Hayworth in familiar glamour-girl pose.

Ginger Rogers catches up on correspondence in the
Writing Room on the *Queen Elizabeth*.

Jack Buchanan, in frivolous mood, borrows the hat and
camera from a New York press photographer.

Gregory Peck and family on deck, as the ship prepares to sail.

GREGORY PECK'S YOUNG SON caused a stir in the nursery one day by hitting his unfortunate playmate over the head with a cricket bat. He must have packed quite a punch as the poor little chap ended up in the ship's hospital with concussion. The blow was apparently not intentional, he was demonstrating his skills as a batsman at the time.

A young fifties starlet, Eleanor Parker, in elegant repose as
the *Queen Elizabeth* steams up the Hudson.

MARLENE DIETRICH was never seen at breakfast, and she would only very occasionally appear for lunch. Whenever she did arrive in the dining-room her entrance was always timed to achieve maximum effect. At midday she would choose to wear very smart tailored two-piece suits with little cloche hats, and in the evening the most glamorous evening dresses, sleek and sophisticated.

She shared her choice of table with Noel Coward, who suggested it, as it was the most prominent position in the dining-room. Although they were great friends, they never travelled at the same time and so never dined together. Marlene heeded Noel's advice, '. . . always be seen darling, always be seen . . .'

Marlene Dietrich, wrapped up against the cold, on board the
Queen Elizabeth in New York.

IN THE EARLY FIFTIES Lord Montgomery, who travelled many times on the *Queen Mary*, requested a visit to the bridge. The ship's officers decided that it would be a good idea to invite him up to the wardroom and, knowing in advance that he preferred not to drink alcohol, they thought that a tea-time invitation would be more appropriate. In addition to his disapproval of the demon drink, it was noted that he abhorred cigarette smoking. All the officers were briefed beforehand and, as a mark of respect to the great man, no one was allowed to smoke in his presence. He arrived at exactly four o'clock and entertained the assembled company with many interesting stories. He had an extensive knowledge of ships, much more than they had given him credit for, and this surprised and delighted many who had been dreading the visit with its customary polite small talk. A very pleasant hour was spent discussing nautical reminiscences and then he took his leave. While he had been chatting Montgomery had noticed that the walls of the wardroom were covered with photographs of the famous people who had visited the ship. He didn't say anything at the time, but later that evening he returned to the wardroom. The first officer answered the door and was somewhat surprised to see him standing outside. Under his arm he was carrying a parcel which he handed over to the young officer saying, 'I thought you might like an addition to your collection, I have brought you this portait of me to hang on your wardroom wall'. Within half an hour it had been placed in a prominent position.

Lord Montgomery posing on deck with actresses
Bonita Granville and Janis Paige.

Mae West struggles with the wind out on deck.

*D*OROTHY LAMOUR always requested her favourite cabin on promenade deck. Some celebrities would not entertain the thought of travelling unless they could ensure a particular suite or cabin.

Jack Benny and Dorothy Lamour in festive mood, in the Observation Lounge on the *Queen Mary*.

Mr and Mrs Henry Ford and friends relax together in the Smoking Room on the *Queen Mary*.

*T*HE ELEGANT and beautiful Tilley Losch was also known as the Countess of Carnarvon.

Tillie Losch, the dancer, rests awhile on the Sun Deck.

Ben Lyon and Bebe Daniels enjoy a refreshing afternoon tea on the Promenade Deck of the *Queen Mary*.

SHIPPING COMPANIES will go to extraordinary lengths to prevent bad publicity. If anyone was unlucky enough to get a media pasting they ran the risk of some of the mud sticking, however true or untrue the allegations were. The popular press has always enjoyed a rather chequered reputation. Facts are often deliberately misrepresented in order to entice the reader to buy the paper. Insinuations and pointed hints have frequently caused irreparable damage to publicly recognized companies, especially those trying to maintain blemish-free records. It is with this in mind that you can perhaps forgive the powers that be for covering up an historic event. It is a little known fact that Wallace Beery, who travelled regularly on the Cunard White Star ships, died on board the *Queen Mary*. A good deal of trouble was taken to prevent the truth leaking to the press. He died two days out to sea *en route* to New York and, after much deliberation, it was decided to smuggle him ashore on arrival. This was achieved with some assistance from dockside workers. He was then booked into a New York Hotel and from there his death was announced a few days later. The fact that he had died from natural causes did nothing to allay fears that this could churn up bad publicity for Cunard and there was a strong possibility that the ensuing public reaction would ultimately affect bookings.

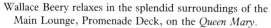

Wallace Beery relaxes in the splendid surroundings of the Main Lounge, Promenade Deck, on the *Queen Mary*.

Bob Hope, Loretta Young, Alexis Smith, Craig Stevens and
Robert Montgomery pose for the camera on the Boat Deck of
the *Queen Mary*.

Raymond Massey strolling along the Boat Deck mid-Atlantic
on the *Queen Elizabeth*.

Ella Fitzgerald at dinner in the first-class restaurant.

Paul Robeson dining in the comfortable surroundings of
the first-class restaurant.

Leo Genn, actor, finds a peaceful corner in the Main Lounge
on the *Queen Elizabeth*.

Arthur Askey rests for a moment
while walking the ship's mile.

Tyrone Power, Jackie Cooper and Hildy Parks line up
behind fellow actors on the Sports Deck.

Moira Lister shows her beautiful satin and lace
evening gown to best advantage.

Burgess Meredith and Paulette Goddard wrapped up warmly
against the bitter cold on the Sports Deck in New York. As
husband and wife, they travelled to Europe regularly.

Valerie Hobson, Mrs John Profumo, relaxing on deck.

Alice Faye and Phil Harris, husband and wife, on their way
up to dinner in the Verandah Grill.

PART 4

THE GOLDEN ERA

1945–1955

RMS *Queen Elizabeth.*

RMS *Queen Mary.*

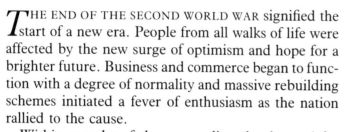

The Golden Era
1945–1955

───────────── ☆ ─────────────

*T*HE END OF THE SECOND WORLD WAR signified the start of a new era. People from all walks of life were affected by the new surge of optimism and hope for a brighter future. Business and commerce began to function with a degree of normality and massive rebuilding schemes initiated a fever of enthusiasm as the nation rallied to the cause.

Within months of the war ending the demand for passage across the Atlantic resumed and the Cunard Line, although proud to have played such an important support role during the war, was now anxious to refurbish both liners and establish them as front runners in the commercial market as soon as possible. There was a great desire to return to the grand old days of transatlantic travel and sample once more the luxury, glamour and excitement of being on board a magnificent ocean liner. It was the beginning of a golden age for Cunard's flagships.

The *Queen Elizabeth*, then over six years old, finally began her maiden voyage when she sailed from Southampton on 16th October 1946. It was not until the following summer, however, that she was joined by her sister ship the *Queen Mary*, thus establishing a joint commercial service for the first time. The thirties saw the advent of the superliners, but the most glamorous and commercially successful period was the decade that stretched from 1945 into the mid-fifties. Cunard reigned supreme, carrying the largest number of transatlantic passengers – at one point over a third of all transatlantic travellers. In 1958, Cunard boasted twelve passenger liners, all offering a service across the Atlantic to the USA and Canada. But of all the passenger liners operating the North Atlantic service, the Queens were not only the most impressive but from the beginning showed immense profits. An established tradition, a reputation for quality and excellence and the prestige of being British gave Cunard the cream of the market – everyone wanted to cross on either the *Queen Elizabeth* or the *Queen Mary*.

*U*P TO THE MID-FIFTIES only salt water baths were available to passengers, even in first class. To have carried enough fresh water to meet the demands of both physical cleanliness and bodily consumption would have destabilized the ship. It was impossible to achieve a reasonable lather using ordinary cosmetic soap so a special salt water soap had to be provided. With the advent of desalination plants the ship was able to take on water directly from the sea and purify it on board.

And so this fervour for extravagant travel continued. Of necessity bookings were always made months in advance, with actresses, politicians, royalty and members of high society all vying with one another to secure the best suite and a table in the Verandah Grill. Sailing days were scenes of organized chaos as the pier-side activities reached a climax of activity: stores were loaded, flowers delivered, luggage sorted and, finally, passengers arrived, in limousines, taxicabs and, in Southampton, on the famous boat-train. All descended in a fever of excitement along the dockside, usually with parties of relatives and well-wishers. In the days before obsessive security guests were allowed on board until half an hour before sailing. This was the time for the grandest celebrations, the Bon Voyage parties! Anyone walking down promenade deck pre-

sailing would be guided past cabins and suites with the sound of popping champagne corks clearly audible through open doors. The passengers would arrange in advance of the sailing date for food and beverages to be placed in the cabin for their sailing party; for the

The Main Lounge, *Queen Elizabeth.*

The Smoking Room, *Queen Elizabeth.*

less well organized these impromptu occasions could be delegated to specialized catering companies.

Just prior to sailing announcements were made for all persons not sailing with the vessel to disembark. As soon as the last gangway was hauled in passengers would line the upper decks, straining to catch a glimpse of their relatives and friends down on the quayside. In keeping with sailing tradition, streamers cascaded down the steel flanks of the ship in a multitude of colours, tangling and muddling as they fell, forming an enormous web of paper ticker-tape which blew away in large clumps as the ship gathered steam down the channel.

A GREAT FRIEND OF Lord Beaverbrook, Sir James Dunn, was a regular patron of Cunard. In addition to his personal tally of annual crossings, his business empire was responsible for an astonishing three million pounds a year in travel fees. Naturally he was elevated to the top ten on the VIP lists and, as a valued customer, he was very well looked after on board. When he travelled he always demanded first-class service and sent advance instructions to ensure a smooth passage. For example, he always requested a particular steward and his favourite waiters to serve at the table (always the same one in the Verandah Grill). On one particular trip he was travelling at the same time as the Duke of Windsor, who was making the crossing from New York to visit his mother, Queen Mary, who had been taken ill. Whenever royalty travelled protocol demanded that their needs and requests took absolute priority. Not long after leaving Pier 90 in New York, a call came through to the purser's office from the restaurant manager of the Verandah Grill seeking assistance to quell a disturbance in the dining-room. On arriving in the Grill, the chief purser observed Sir James Dunn standing by the Duke of Windsor's table in an angry mood, behaving in a less than respectful manner. He had the attention of everyone in the room, which was packed to capacity as the lunchtime service was in full swing. The chief purser, Mr Carine, who was known as the diplomat of the western ocean, stepped forward to tackle the delicate problem. Although Sir James was a valued customer he was obviously causing a great deal of embarrassment to the Duke of Windsor, in particular by suggesting loudly that he had let his country down and that he was a disgrace to the empire. Mr Carine spoke quietly and politely to Sir James and pointed out that the Duke of Windsor was still a member of the royal family and as such must be afforded all the privileges of his rank and status, especially when travelling with the most senior British merchant shipping company. It transpired that the Duke of Windsor had been given Sir James' regular table and that sparked off the verbal attack. Having assessed the situation, Mr Carine then asked Sir James to apologize to His Royal Highness and quietly suggested that if he did not do so immediately his bags would be removed and taken down to 'R' deck, where they would be disembarked, with his good self and all his retinue, on to the Ambrose channel light vessel, which was due to rendezvous with the liner in an hour's time. After an uncomfortably long pause, and a few grumbles, Sir James conceded defeat and apologized to the Duke. A huge sigh of relief went round the dining-room and many passengers came forward to congratulate Mr Carine, who had so successfully and tactfully defused the situation. The Duke later thanked the chief purser for his admirable skill in dealing with a difficult problem.

*T*HE LIST BELOW SHOWS the astonishing quantity of food needed on board for one voyage of the *Queen Mary*. This selection represents a typical example of the variety of basic ingredients used on a specific crossing: 4th May 1956.

Biscuits	1,100 lbs
Cereals	1,800 lbs
Beans and peas, dried	950 lbs
Flour, all kinds	20,000 lbs
Macaroni, spaghetti, etc	550 lbs
Oatmeal and rolled oats	450 lbs
Dried fruits	1,300 lbs
Fish, canned	1,150 lbs
Fruit canned, two sizes	2,650 cans
Mustards, various	150 lbs
Peppers, spices and herbs	150 lbs
Salt	2,400 lbs
Fruit conserves	35 lbs
Preserved honey and ginger	45 lbs
Jams and marmalade, 1 lb	1,050 jars
Jams and marmalade, 7 lbs	75 cans
Jellies, various	115 lbs
Syrups, various	30 gallons
Juices, fruit and vegetable	2,750 cans
Nuts, various	550 lbs
Pickles and olives	800 bottles
Sauces, ketchups, chutneys	900 bottles
Salad oil	160 gallons
Turtle soups	475 pints
Drinking chocolate, cocoa	41 lbs
Coffee, various brands	1,700 lbs
Sugar, cubes, granulated, etc	7,500 lbs
Teas, various	1,100 lbs
Vinegars	900 pints

Vegetables, canned and purée	3,500 cans
Strained foods, infants	300 cans
Essences	25 bottles
Bacon	5,150 lbs
Hams	2,500 lbs
Cheeses	1,800 lbs
Butter	5,900 lbs
Eggs	70,250 no
Cream	3,250 qts
Milk, fresh	24,250 pints
Milk, evaporated	600 gallons
Margarine and lard	2,250 lbs
Fish, fresh and shell	19,500 lbs
Fish, smoked	1,450 lbs
Salmon, smoked scotch	425 lbs
Sturgeon, smoked	50 lbs
Snails	300 lbs
Scallops and clams	125 gallons
Apples, 40 lb boxes	300 boxes
Apricots, dessert	100 lbs
Bananas	1,450 lbs
Blueberries	100 lbs
Grapes, mixed	1,500 lbs
Grapefruit	90 boxes
Lemons	35 boxes
Limes	1,000 no
Melons, various	2,800 no
Nectarines	300 no
Oranges, various	18,000 no
Tangerines	100 lbs
Peaches	500 no
Pears, various	1,150 lbs
Pineapples	75 no
Strawberries, fresh	2,250 lbs
Soft fruits, other	1,500 lbs
Ice-cream	4,000 qts
Choice loins of beef	1,900 lbs

Choice ribs of beef	1,250 lbs
Choice fillets of beef	1,150 lbs
Beef, various	2,000 lbs
Beef, corned	1,500 lbs
Lamb, including joints	10,100 lbs
Pork, including joints	2,500 lbs
Pork, corned	850 lbs
Veal	1,850 lbs
Offals, various	3,650 lbs
Tongues, corned and smoked	1,250 lbs
Chickens, broiling	1,900 lbs
Chickens, squab	175 lbs
Chickens, Guinea	115 lbs
Chickens, roasting	6,500 lbs
Chickens, poussins	90 lbs
Poulardes de bresse	900 lbs
Poulets de grain	600 lbs
Pigeons, various	425 lbs
Turkeys, tom	5,950 lbs
Turkeys, hen	225 lbs
Turkeys, smoked	50 lbs
Sausages, breakfast, etc	2,150 lbs
Vegetables	41,000 lbs
Vegetables, frozen	8,750 lbs
Potatoes	55,000 lbs
Other specialities, caviare, foie gras, etc	1,000 lbs

Special requirements carried at all times to cover: kosher meals, specific dietary needs and Japanese and Chinese stores.

MANY DIFFERENT RELIGIOUS groups travelled on the Queens. In some cases, a large group from a particular area, from Boston or Chicago for example, would embark *en masse* for the voyage. Some Roman Catholics were unhappy that Mass was held in the cinema and not in the main lounge; some felt strongly enough to voice their opinions loudly to the Cunard management. Realizing that the morning service was given more priority on other shipping lines, Cunard was quick to comply with their requests and Mass was held in the main lounge at 9:30 am as opposed to 10:00 am in the cinema. Changes take time to filter through the system and, unfortunately, some of the original notices giving the times of the services were accidently left on display around the ship. This did not please Spencer Tracey, who arrived at the purser's office one morning in a furious temper because he had missed the morning service. He had read the wrong information from one of the old notices.

WHEN THE DUKE OF WINDSOR was travelling with his sister, the Princess Royal, he expressed a wish to try his hand at the daily competition. These were written tests, with a crossword- clue format, using the passenger lists to find the answer to the clues. The Chambers dictionary was used instead of the Oxford dictionary, as there was usually a high percentage of American passengers. One of the regular clues used was, 'an old Scottish coin'. At six o'clock each day the winning answers were posted up on a board near the purser's office. The Duke loved to win these competitions and he always claimed his prize – a rather ordinary tankard. One evening the Duke came down to check his answers against the board and realizing that he had not won asked to speak to the chief purser. He expressed his disappointment at not winning and the purser replied, 'Never mind Sir, you can't win them all, and you have got enough tankards already, surely you can't possibly want any more!' The Duke said that he felt sure he had won, and did not agree with the solution given to the 'old Scottish coin' clue. The purser explained that the answer had been taken from the Chambers dictionary which was the usual source of clues in the competition. The Duke then said, 'Since when was the Chambers dictionary an authority on old Scottish coins? I am certain my answer is right, and I should know better than any American dictionary!' 'How is that Sir?' asked the purser. The Duke replied, 'Remember young man, I was once the King of Scotland!'

As soon as a ship leaves port the quayside becomes a quiet, vacuous place. Out at sea, however, a different atmosphere prevails from the moment the vessel leaves the pier and new friendships are already being formed in what has become a thriving 'island' community. The magic and mystique of being at sea is accentuated by the mode of transportation – one of the most luxurious and majestic ships afloat. In addition there is always the thrill of rubbing shoulders with one of the many celebrities on board. The exhilarating experience of being in close proximity to a famous film star, politician or member of the royal family for an extended period of time made travelling on the Queens particularly memorable.

PRINCE AKAHITO was a table-tennis player of world-class standard and was always keen to play in the ship's competition. As his victory was always a foregone conclusion, the purser went to the captain and asked whether they should present him with a special prize as opposed to the usual tankard

Captain Sorrell acknowledges the cheers as the *Queen Mary* sails into New York.

DURING A TUG STRIKE in New York in the early fifties the *Caronia*, another Cunard ship, attempted to dock alongside Pier 90 without tug assistance. As the ship approached the south side of the pier the breeze took her a little off course and she rammed the end of the pier. She did eventually make a successful docking after several attempts. This would probably have faded into insignificance had it not been for the arrival of the *Queen Mary* the very next morning. Undaunted by the lack of tugs, Captain Sorrell manoeuvred the giant liner into a turn slightly upstream of her intended berth on the north side of Pier 90. The operation was watched by the entire crew of the rather dented

Caronia, as well as thousands of passers by on shore, including drivers who had stopped their cars in order to get a better view, causing one of the biggest traffic jams New York had seen. Everyone held their breath as the *Queen Mary* slowly came about and as her bows swung round she drifted gracefully downstream. As soon as she was on line Captain Sorrell manoeuvred her gently into her berth without any mishap. There followed bursts of applause and whoops of delight from an admiring crowd, with car horns and boat sirens sounding in the background. This was a remarkable achievement and worthy of a place of honour in the record books.

The Observation Lounge and Cocktail Bar,
Queen Elizabeth.

engraving. All this was happening not long after the war, so not surprisingly the Prince was extremely displeased to be presented with a tankard showing a hangman and inscribed 'The Last Drop'. The ensuing adverse reaction to this unforgiveable *faux pas* escalated into a major incident, the repercussions of which eventually hit the national press on both sides of the Atlantic.

The decade from 1945 to 1955 corresponded with a time when quality and impeccable service were *de rigueur*. Companies were determined to stay at the top of their particular sphere of interest and this pre-eminence was achieved through hard work and well-earned merit. In the big shipping lines crew members were proud of their uniforms and what they stood for; a Cunard man stood out from a Union Castle man, who in turn was proud to be different from a P&O man. Crew turnover was considerably lower than in the same business today, and high morale and a keen sense of duty prevailed on board.

Cunard managed to achieve an unbroken record of harmony throughout this travelling heyday and ran an impressive and enviable operation. Passengers would invariably patronize a happy, well-run ship and Cunard's impressive figures during the period from 1945 to 1955 are testimony to that. The company enjoyed many bountiful years and the two Queens led the field and successfully reaped the harvest on the North Atlantic. For Cunard, it really was the Golden Age of Transatlantic Travel.

bearing an engraved slogan. The captain suggested that no special provision should be made and that he should receive the same prize as any other passenger. The final match was played in the main lounge instead of the promenade deck, where the tables were permanently set up. Nobody was surprised when the Prince stormed to victory. As he stepped forward to collect his prize the chief purser, thinking quickly, turned the tankard over to make sure that the 'slogan' was not an offensive one. To this horror he realized that the captain was about to present a tankard with a most unsuitable

Sir Winston Churchill arriving on board with his entourage.

Mr and Mrs Anthony Eden with 'Rab' Butler and his wife
prior to disembarking in New York.

*B*EFORE GOING TO SLEEP Sir Winston Churchill would sit up in bed reading while puffing on one of his enormous cigars. His ever watchful room steward was so concerned about the potential fire risk that he designed a contraption, which, with the co-operation of Sir Winston proved very effective.

If he fell asleep while smoking the cigar would roll down a cunningly placed fire resistant shute and be extinguished after falling into a bucket full of water by his bed. This primitive device proved to be an effective fire deterrent on several occasions.

Queen Soraya of Persia absorbed in a game of backgammon
with the Shah's brother in the Smoking Room on
the *Queen Mary*.

The Shah of Persia on the bridge of the *Queen Mary* with
Captain Donald Sorrell and a fellow officer.

WHEN THE SHAH OF PERSIA came to England with his wife Queen Soraya an official reception was held prior to his embarkation on board the *Queen Mary*. A gun salute resounded from the ramparts of the fort at the entrance to Portsmouth harbour, timed to coincide with the ship as she made her way down the Solent.

SOME FAMOUS PASSENGERS allowed certain members of the crew to visit their cabins in order to view the contents of their travelling wardrobes. The doors of Queen Soraya's closets were flung wide to reveal a staggering quantity of clothes, the most luxurious fabrics and the most exquisite shoes and accessories. It was noted that she never repeated an outfit twice, and that she changed regularly throughout the day. She was a lady of great beauty and these adornments served to enhance her natural charisma. Her arrival in the dining-room each evening was an event not to be missed.

*H*ERMIONE GINGOLD was a frequent traveller who had a reputation for the quick retort. On one occasion, towards the end of the *Queen Mary*'s commercial service, Miss Gingold awaited her order for breakfast. The stewards had been collecting large quantities of soiled linen to go ashore on arrival and as a result her breakfast arrived with a paper napkin folded on the tray. She looked at it in horror and turned to her bedroom steward saying, 'What is this place . . . Joe Lyons with fins?'

Fernandel on the Boat Deck of the *Queen Elizabeth* prior to sailing from New York.

Hermione Gingold assists the purser in the Main Lounge on the *Queen Elizabeth*.

*O*N ARRIVAL IN SOUTHAMPTON Hermione Gingold was being interviewed on deck by local reporters. One of them asked her how she liked living in New York. Miss Gingold replied, 'I love it, I adore it . . . I love the atmosphere, the wonderful skyline and that magnificent statue of Dame Judith Anderson holding a cigarette lighter.'

LORD AND LADY DOCKER, frequent passengers on the transatlantic route, were prominent socialites. One story goes that they were offended not to be invited to the royal wedding of Princess Margaret to Anthony Armstrong-Jones. Rather than face up to this social snub, they hatched a plan whereby it would appear impossible for them to attend. They booked a return ticket on the *Queen Mary*, under the name 'Mr and Mrs Smith'. They travelled across to New York, stayed on board and came straight back again on the return voyage. Thus, they were 'out of the country' at the time of the wedding and anyone noticing their absence would put it down to prior commitments, or more pressing social engagements. Unfortunately they overlooked the inevitability of being recognized by members of the crew.

☆

THE DOCKERS would automatically be placed on the ship's VIP list and would attend private parties as well as the captain's parties and receptions. They would also host their own private parties, which occasionally would get a little rowdy. On one occasion an unsuspecting waiter was soaked to the skin by the contents of an ice bucket.

☆

LADY DOCKER travelled with her lady companion, but sometimes Sir Bernard and her son Lance accompanied the party. They were invited to the captain's cabin for cocktails one evening and on arrival Lady Docker noticed a signed photograph of President Tito displayed on the wall. She grabbed the frame and threw it on the floor, smashing the glass. 'How dare you have that communist —— in your cabin', she shouted at the captain. All the guests were flabbergasted by this outburst, and the captain's steward was forced to ask Her Ladyship to leave. As she flounced out of the cabin, she turned and made a final appropriate gesture in the air at the shocked party.

☆

PRIOR TO MOST MEALS, Lady Docker would send down her order from the menu in advance. She not only made a selection, but duplicated the order so that everyone at her table ate the same, regardless of their preference. Her favourite food was leg of lamb, or rack of lamb, with either plain salad or simply cooked vegetables and, although her favourite tipple was vodka, which she often drank with her meal, there was always an abundant supply of the very best champagne on the table. She was known to have a highly volatile temperament but Lady Docker was a very popular passenger on board and she frequently gave generous gratuities to those who had served her well. Her table steward, an Irishman called Gerry, had built up a special rapport with her. One evening he noticed a very handsome solid gold cigarette case lying on the table in front of her. Lady Docker caught his admiring gaze, and said, 'Gerry, do you like that?' Gerry was caught unawares. 'Yes, Madam, I think it's beautiful', he stammered. Her Ladyship replied, 'You're right it is, that old bastard over there bought it for me!' And she nodded in the direction of Sir Bernard, 'But you must have it as a gift, I insist.'

Sir Bernard and Lady Docker relax with a cocktail in
the Dance Salon on the *Queen Elizabeth*.

Cecil Beaton, society photographer, caught on the other side
of the camera, as he strolls the deck on the *Queen Mary*.

Lillian Gish and Constance Collyer, recently arrived on
board, inspecting one of their suites.

Tennessee Williams, the playwright, in the first-class restaurant on the *Queen Mary*. Note the locating rope stanchion attached to the underside of the chair, a necessary precaution in rough weather.

Duke Ellington on the Boat Deck of the *Queen Elizabeth*, mid-Atlantic.

Hoagy Carmichael and his wife enjoy the wide open spaces of
the Sports Deck on the *Queen Elizabeth*.

*H*OAGY CARMICHAEL made frequent crossings
on the Queens during the war years in his
capacity as a troop entertainer. On one crossing to
New York the ship hit a freak wave which did some
considerable damage to the bows and the forward
deck. When the weather had improved a little, all
hands were called forward to the affected area to
assist in a clearing-up operation. Word soon spread
that one of the most willing 'hands' on deck was
none other than Hoagy himself.

Pearl Bailey, the cabaret star, in the Main Lounge on
the *Queen Elizabeth*.

Yehudi Menuhin and his wife dine in the exclusive
Verandah Grill on the *Queen Mary*.

Mr and Mrs Artur Rubinstein at dinner in the first-class
restaurant on the *Queen Elizabeth*.

Charles Chaplin and his wife Oona entertain guests in the
Dance Salon on the *Queen Elizabeth*.

The Woolworth heiress, Barbara Hutton, finding peace and
solitude on the Promenade Deck of the *Queen Mary*.

Walt Disney and family enjoy an evening in the Dance Salon
on the *Queen Elizabeth*.

*B*ARBARA HUTTON, the Woolworth heiress, was
hardly ever seen in public when on board. She
preferred to remain in her suite, occasionally
venturing out on deck to take some exercise and
fresh air. On one particular crossing, whilst
ascending the stairs, she was in collision with a
waiter who was racing down on some urgent errand.
He apologized profusely but Barbara Hutton could
not have been more charming: 'It's quite alright,
you have your work to do, and I'm only on vacation,
think nothing of it'.

*W*ALT DISNEY and his family always booked
a particular table by the window in the
Verandah Grill restaurant. The regular sailing time
for the Queens from New York coincided with the
sunset behind the Manhattan skyline and, as this
spectacular scene was a firm favourite with the
Disney family, they would always reserve the same
spot.

Charles Boyer and Spencer Tracey in deep conversation on
the Promenade Deck, *Queen Mary*.

Herbert Marshall, the actor with his wife in the
Observation Bar on the *Queen Mary*.

Michael Wilding and Elizabeth Taylor playing
housey-housey in the Main Lounge.

*E*LIZABETH TAYLOR often travelled with her canine companions. She would send regular orders to the kitchen where the fish chef, Archie Pirre, would prepare special food for them. This was in addition to the elaborate dinners prepared for herself and delivered to the suite that she shared with Nicky Hilton, to whom she was married at the time.

☆

*E*LIZABETH TAYLOR liked to walk the decks to exercise her dog. One day a crew member saw her and plucked up the courage to speak to her. 'What is his name?', he asked, looking at her small white poodle. '**HIS** name is Tessa', she replied, and gave him a dazzling smile!

☆

*E*LIZABETH TAYLOR and Nicky Hilton began their honeymoon on board the *Queen Elizabeth*. Fellow passengers and ever watchful crew were somewhat surprised, on the first evening, to observe Nicky Hilton in the smoking-room playing cards, where he stayed until the early hours of the morning. So much for the ultimate romantic trip across the Atlantic.

☆

*B*EFORE MIKE TODD was killed, he and Elizabeth Taylor used to travel regularly. On their last trip to England together they were spotted in the main foyer of The Dorchester hotel. All the principal staff, page boys and management were assembled in line as a mark of respect. Mike Todd went along the line thanking each one in turn, distributing five pound notes like confetti.

Elizabeth Taylor poses with one of her dogs on the Sports Deck, *Queen Mary*.

Richard Burton and Elizabeth Taylor in a rare picture with Debbie Reynolds.

RICHARD BURTON and Elizabeth Taylor were chatting in the wardroom to the staff captain. They were discussing the movie to be shown on board that evening which was scheduled to be the epic *Anne Boleyn*. Although Richard was the star of the film he had no particular desire to see it and asked the staff captain if he would accompany Elizabeth to the show. The officer was delighted and later that evening he proudly escorted Miss Taylor into the cinema. It didn't take long for the news to travel round the auditorium that Elizabeth Taylor was present and gradually everyone began to turn round. Soon there were more people watching her than the film itself, much to the embarrassment of her escort.

Oskar Homolka, actor/director, with his wife Joan Tetzel on
the *Queen Elizabeth*.

Myrna Loy and Gene Markey enjoy dinner in the first-class
restaurant on the *Queen Elizabeth*.

Jerry Lewis and Dean Martin with the actor Sessue
Hayakawa, who played the Japanese Commander in
Bridge on the River Kwai.

ON ONE CROSSING Dean Martin and Jerry Lewis were travelling to Europe with their party of guests. It was an excellent trip and they had put on a show for the passengers and crew which had been much enjoyed. It was during dinner one evening that an Irishman, a little the worse for drink, suddenly jumped up from his chair and grabbing a water jug threw its contents into the middle of the room. He then started shouting and yelling anti-Jewish slogans while running amok between the tables. It didn't take long for the restaurant manager and chief purser to spring into action, and Dean Martin and Jerry Lewis joined in the chase. It was like a scene from the Keystone Cops, as grown men raced around the restaurant all trying to catch the drunken Irishman who managed to outwit them all for several minutes. He dived out of sight under tables and, had it not been for the startled expressions on some of the female passengers' faces, he might never have been caught! Finally, he was brought down with legs and arms flailing, still hurling abuse at the top of his voice. The master at arms and the officer of the watch were summoned and they took him away and locked him up until he was sober enought to be set free. A loud cheer greeted the celebrity challengers, and once more order was restored in the dining-room.

Judy Garland enjoys the fresh sea breezes on the open deck.

Cary Grant in the first-class dining-room on the
Queen Mary with Binnie Barnes and her daughter.
Her husband was then head of Columbia Pictures.

CARY GRANT loved the *Queen Mary*. He would always endeavour to time his journeys across the Atlantic to coincide with the sailing schedule of his favourite ship. He would describe her to his friends in the most glowing terms; his favourite expression was, 'The *Queen Mary* is the eighth wonder of the world.'

BINNIE BARNES, a popular socialite, also loved to dance the night away. One evening she was being wooed by a rather handsome millionaire, who, in his enthusiasm, kept tipping the band one hundred dollar bills to keep playing her favourite tunes. At the end of the evening he was rather hoping for something more than a goodnight kiss. However, his amorous advances were apparently unrewarded as the following morning he went back to the lounge and asked the band to return all his money! The ship's musicians were obviously an understanding bunch because they gave back every penny, over one thousand dollars.

Noel Coward relaxes with a brandy in the Smoking Room on
the *Queen Mary*.

NOEL COWARD was one of the most frequent travellers on the Queens. He was extremely popular with passengers and crew for his great sense of humour and all-round social grace. He was travelling across on one occasion and was engaged in conversation with Clifton Webb, who had recently lost his mother. During the course of the discussion the reminiscences about his mother brought tears to the ageing actor's eyes. True to form, Noel Coward retorted, 'The one thing I cannot stand are these deplorable tears from a seventy-six-year-old orphan.'

Deborah Kerr enjoys afternoon tea with her young daughter
in the Main Lounge on the *Queen Mary*.

Michael Redgrave about to go up to the Sports Deck
and take in some fresh sea air.

Mary Martin chats with fellow passengers on the
Boat Deck, *Queen Mary*.

Ivor Novello, composer and actor, with friends at dinner in
the first-class dining-room on the *Queen Elizabeth*.

Actress Glynis Johns relaxing in the Dance Salon on
the *Queen Elizabeth*.

Paul Munie on his way to the dining-room on
the *Queen Mary*.

After five days at sea the sight of land brings everyone out on
deck, and David Farrar, John Mills, and their families
look for familiar landmarks.

*J*OHN MILLS delighted in visiting the bridge whenever he was on board. On one occasion he was invited up by Captain Sorrell and during the visit he spoke of the many sea adventure films he had made over the years. These experiences had made him feel quite at home with the ship's officers and he joked about taking over the bridge and giving them all a rest.

Vera Lynn, the 'forces' sweetheart', dining in the elegant
first-class restaurant on the *Queen Elizabeth*.

Claire Bloom looking radiant, at dinner in the first-class
restaurant on the *Queen Elizabeth*.

Ray Milland with his wife, shortly after boarding
in New York.

Terence Rattigan relaxing with a book on the
Promenade Deck of the *Queen Mary*.

Robert Taylor with his beautiful second wife, Ursula Thiess,
at dinner in the first-class restaurant.

Bonita Granville and Jack Wrather host an auction in the
Smoking Room on the *Queen Elizabeth*.

PART 5

EPILOGUE

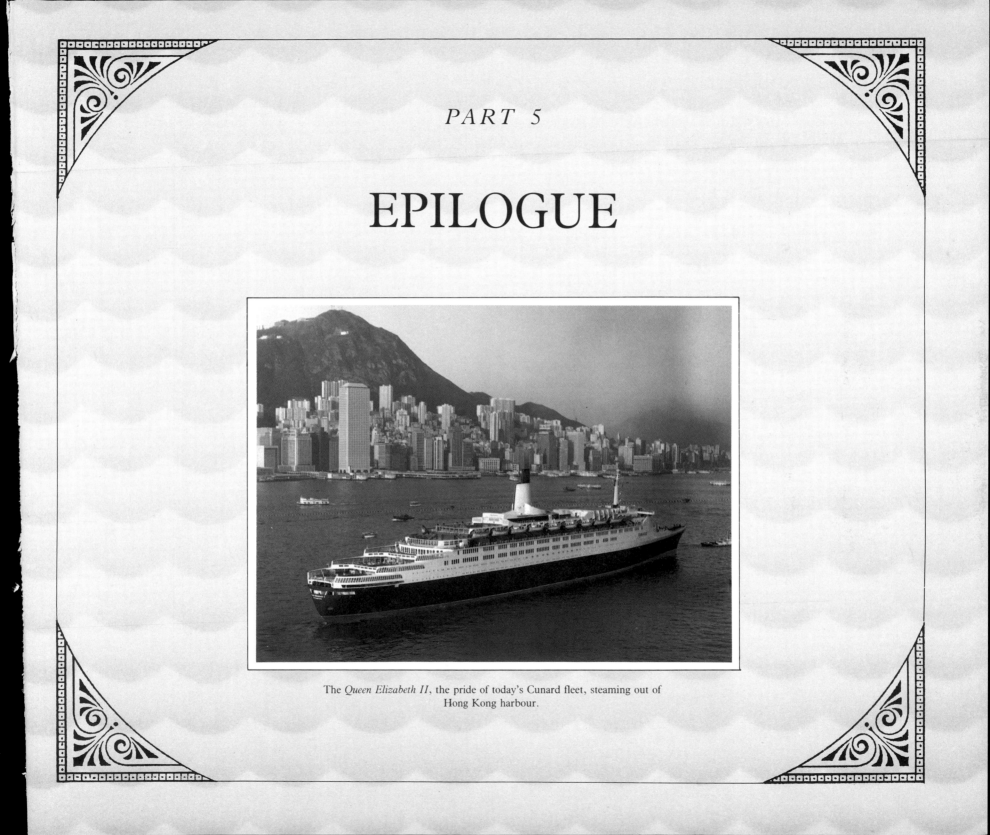

The *Queen Elizabeth II*, the pride of today's Cunard fleet, steaming out of Hong Kong harbour.

Epilogue

─────────── ☆ ───────────

BY THE LATE FIFTIES the growth of commercial air travel was beginning to eat into the passenger market across the Atlantic. The great Cunard liners no longer held the monopoly and when fuel price rises exacerbated the situation something radical had to be done to stem the flow of revenue from the Cunard coffers. It was decided to transfer the *Queen Elizabeth* to the potentially more lucrative cruise circuit and in 1965 she entered dry dock for a major overhaul. This move was intended to ensure her service life for at least the next decade. Despite the rather bearish market Cunard were planning to build a third liner to replace the *Queen Mary*.

The refurbishments to the *Queen Elizabeth* included the installation of much needed air-conditioning, new plumbing and the addition of a large swimming pool on the stern lido deck. Sadly, in spite of all efforts to attract a new market, passenger figures continued to show poor returns and the new cruising schedule proved to be a financial disaster.

At the end of one particular season, when both Queens lost large amounts of revenue, a decision was taken to retire the *Queen Mary* from service. It seemed then only a matter of time before the *Queen Elizabeth* would follow her sister ship into retirement. Neither ship had been built for cruising; both found it difficult to berth in many of the ports of call because of their size. After several years of decline and multi-million dollar losses, it was regrettably decided that they would both have to be sold.

The winning bid for the *Queen Mary* came from Long Beach, California. This go-ahead American city planned to convert the ship into a floating tourist attraction, with hotel facilities and a maritime museum. She was sold for $3.45 million – a bargain when one considers that years later an overhaul on the *QE2* cost Cunard over £90 million.

On 31st October 1967, the *Queen Mary* once again attracted world-wide attention as she began her last voyage and Atlantic crossing. She departed from Southampton on a thirty-nine-day voyage that was billed as her 'Last Great Cruise'. Thousands of people turned out to see her off from her home port, while Royal Navy helicopters flew overhead in a giant anchor formation. The sea was packed with small vessels and craft, all blowing their horns and whistles, streamers

The *Queen Elizabeth* ablaze in Hong Kong harbour. She sank
on 9th January 1972.

flew and balloons were released. The *Queen Mary* herself boasted a 310–foot paying-off pennant, ten feet for every year of service, proudly flying from her main mast. The voyage covered 14,559 miles and took her around Cape Horn where she created a new record –

the largest passenger ship to carry the greatest number of passengers around the Cape.

For a time the *Queen Elizabeth* looked set to join her sister ship in America, for she was bought by an American who took her to Port Everglades. She too was to be reincarnated as a floating hotel. But plans did not come to fruition and, after lying idle for two years, she was sold to the Taiwanese shipping magnate CY Tung. Her new owner wanted to convert her into a floating university that would eventually tour the world. She was renamed *Seawise University* and sailed to Hong Kong for a refit.

In 1972, following a $6 million overhaul, she caught fire while lying at anchor in Hong Kong harbour. The fire raged out of control for two days and, despite the efforts of the fire crews, she finally capsized. She remained in the harbour for nearly a year – a giant hulk of grotesquely twisted metal – until she was broken up and sold off for scrap. A sad end to a ship which had become synonymous with stylish luxury afloat.

It became clear to Cunard that for a new liner to be financially viable she must be versatile. No more single-purpose ships, constructed for one market and one specific schedule. An all-weather, highly manoeuvrable, well-equipped superliner, with the ability to adjust to flexible operating schedules was the ship of the future. This new breed of superliner would be highly automated, equipped with the latest technology and be economical to operate. There was much speculation about the name of the new ship and she was known for some time as Q3. Eventually, her name was chosen, and in 1969 the *Queen Elizabeth II*, last in a long line of thoroughbred liners, was launched on the Clyde.

The great Cunard tradition continues today with the *QE2*, the last ship of a lost era, and currently the only liner to offer a transatlantic service to America and back. Whilst she is very far removed from the nostalgic vision of the first transatlantic Queens, she admirably fulfills the needs of passengers in the 1980s. The Cunard catch-phrase tells us that 'Getting there is half the fun!' The contents of this book testify to that.

ACKNOWLEDGEMENTS

I would like to thank the following people for taking the time to talk to me and for providing material for the book:

Stuart Hunter-Cox for his unfailing support and encouragement when I needed it most; David Biggs and Robin Davies of Cunard Line Ltd for some of the marvellous Cunard memorabilia; John Marven; Ian Ferguson; Captain Mortimer Hehir; Oscar Bassam of the Park Lane Hotel; Robin Edwards; John Bainbridge; Alex Callaghan; John Dooley; Mike Kelly; Moyra Connolly; Muriel Arnold; Dianne Coles; the Southampton Maritime Museum; Captain Peter Jackson; LG Hunter-Cox; PJ Hunter-Cox; Alyson Gregory who edited the book and Vic Giolitto and Malcolm Couch the designers. Finally my thanks to Burt and Vera Mason whose enthusiasm fired my imagination and got me to first base.